JUST HOWL

By: Lynn Leite

By Lynn Leite

Copyright © by Lynn Leite

This is a work of fiction. Names, characters, places and incidents are the product of the author's imagination or are used fictitiously, and any resemblance to actual persons living or dead events or locals is purely coincidental.

By Lynn Leite

1

The phone's Caller ID said Waylon. Emerald took a deep breath before answering. It was her job at the Pack house to answer phones, go through emails, and judge whether a request was urgent or not. It was a lot of responsibility for a Human assistant to the Alpha of the Blue Rock Pack, but she loved it.

"Mommy, the phone winging," her three-year-old Gwen reminded.

"I know, Honey," she smiled at Gwen, who was covered in washable paint that the Alpha's second, Nico, had bought her.

Looking at the phone like it might bite, she picked it up. "Good morning, Mayor Blake's office, can I help you?" she said cheerfully.

The Mayor Blake part of the greeting was strictly for any random humans that might call the number.

"You can ask Nico to come to the phone," the woman on the other end snapped.

The Caller ID said Waylon, but it was always Cora looking for Nico on the other end of the line.

"I've told you a thousand times. I'm not his secretary, Cora."

"He is not answering his cell phone."

"Could it be that he doesn't want to speak to you?" Emerald had had enough. Nico's love life gave her more aggravation than any other part of the job. Cora was the worst. She was not all there in the head. Nico swore he only went out with her once and he hadn't slept with her.

"He can't avoid me forever," she screamed and hung up.

"Mommy, no more boo," Gwen whined.

"Mr. Nico can buy you more blue. Why don't you go find him and tell him, make sure to give him a big hug?"

Nico was the Alpha's second and lived in the Pack house, along with Blake and his mate, Alice. Gwen hugging him with paint on her hands would be partial payback for having to field Cora's calls.

Despite having poor judgment when it came to dating, the man was a godsend when it came to Gwen. He was so good with her. The man would make one hell of a father one day, if he ever found his mate. Until then, Emerald would turn away at least one woman a day who was hoping that Nico was the one. His constant parade of women was the only thing keeping Emerald from wishing he was hers.

"You did that on purpose," Nico came from the other room with Gwen on his hip. Tiny hand prints were all over his shirt and even on his face.

"She was out of blue. You are the one that bought the paints." Emerald was trying to keep a straight face.

"Kids love paints."

"And Moms, not so much," Emerald shrugged. "Cora called again. She said you can't avoid her forever."

"I can try."

"We told you that dating multiple women at one time was going to come back to bite you."

"Thankfully, none of them has tried to bite," Nico laughed, putting Gwen down to play. "None of them were my mate. All of them were shifters. I figured they would understand."

"You forgot the most important thing."

"What?"

"They were female. I'm just a lowly human trying to understand the Shifter culture, but I do know that, shifter or not, women are women. We want the right guy, the one that will stick. Those women you are dating don't want to compete. They are looking for love and commitment. At least, most of them are. I can see the hope in their eyes when they come here so you can take them out. Have you ever just picked a woman up and took her to dinner, kissed her goodnight, and called the next day?"

"Life isn't a Hallmark movie. They know I'm not theirs."

"Do they? Then, why do they keep calling? Alice told me she didn't know for months that Blake was hers."

"You have a point."

"I know I do. I'm not criticizing your choice to have a harem, or is it stable?"

"Stable is for prostitutes," Nico joked.

"Pross a toots?" Gwen chimed.

"Wonderful, Gwen, can you bring this to Ms. Alice?" Emerald had gathered some Mating requests that Alice was asked to go over as a formality. She put them in an envelope so they didn't get paint on them and handed it to Gwen, who toddled down the hall.

"Sorry about that."

"She's like a parrot. She repeats everything. Nico, I'm concerned about you."

"Because you care. Maybe, you are my mate?"

"Maybe, I don't want to be another notch on your bedpost."

"If you were mine, you'd be the last notch."

"Very funny, Cora is dangerous. Are you sure she doesn't think you are her mate? I heard it could be one-sided."

"She wishes I was hers, but I don't think she seriously believes I am. She knows I'm not exclusive and, for your information, my bedpost is notch-less."

"That is only because you go to their place."

"I was never intimate with Cora. Emerald, I don't sleep with all of them. Some of the other women just want to have a good time."

"I'm glad to hear about Cora. Maybe that's why she keeps calling. She wants you in her bed. I just wanted to have a good time once in my life. Gwen is the result. I wouldn't trade her for anything, but my point is there are consequences to reckless behavior."

"Unmated shifters rarely get pregnant. It's a Shifter thing and I don't date humans."

"I'd be insulted, but I'm more relieved," Emerald said, seeing Gwen was on her way back.

"I'd rock your world," Nico joked.

"I don't doubt it," Emerald smiled, throwing him off his game. He was sure she would argue. "I just want other things. Things I don't think you could deliver. I had exactly one *one-night stand* in my life. I got the most precious gift anyone could ask for, but I feel like it short-changed her."

"How so? You're a great Mom."

"She doesn't have a Dad. You are wonderful with her and I am grateful. Blake and Alice have stepped up as sort of godparents. I feel like if something happened to me, you would all take care of her and that's more than I had for the first three years. One day, you will have your own, so will Alice and Blake."

"I will still be there for Gwen."

"I know and I thank you. If and when I ever decide to date, I'm not picking a man with five other women in his rotation."

"I've cut back. There are only three," Nico smirked

"You know what I mean," Emerald smiled.

"I do. I will talk to Cora and, hopefully, find a mate sooner rather than later."

"Do you really want a mate?""

"More than anything, does that surprise you?"

"I always said you be a great Dad but a lousy husband."

"When I find her, that's it. My past, her past, it all won't matter. Shifters mate for life, Emerald."

"Then, I hope to hell it isn't Cora."

"You and me both."

2

"Oh shit," Nico groaned.

He and a few of the Pack guards were out having drinks at the local dive. The Den wasn't really a dive, but it looked like it from the outside to discourage humans from entering. There were humans in the bar area and the restaurant, but they were pack and knew about shifters. It was the random tourists they were trying to avoid.

"What?" Jett asked looking at his friend.

Nico, at one time, had been the leader of the guard. Blake had been the Alpha second until the former Alpha passed with no heirs months ago. Now, Nico was the Alpha's second and Blake had been thrust into taking over as Alpha. Eli had taken Nico's former position and all three of them were getting used to the new Pack hierarchy.

"Cora." That was all Nico had to say before the woman spotted him.

"You and I need to talk," she called from across the room, pushing people out of the way.

"Then, talk." Nico leaned back in his chair, looking calmer than he felt.

"You were supposed to call me back. I left ten messages with that Human bitch."

Normally, the word bitch describing a Shifter female was acceptable. The term had been banned from the Pack house because of three-year-old Gwen. Calling a human a bitch was a whole other thing.

"First of all, have some respect. Emerald is human and the Alpha's assistant. She is not my secretary. You can't call the Pack house every time I don't call you back."

"Then, call me back."

The three men made a hushed sound and leaned back in their own chairs. *"Hell hath no fury like a woman scorned"* was muttered under Cole's breath. Nico would have yelled at him, but he was right. Cora was unhinged.

"Cora, I don't want to call you back. I'm looking for my mate and you are not her."

"Since when?"

"Since when was I looking, or since when was it not you?"

"Both."

"I've always been looking, like most of the males and females in here." Nico knew they had gathered an audience. "You are not my mate. A friend recently pointed out that I should be focusing on my goal rather than having a good time."

"I was just a good time?" the woman screeched.

"I'm trying to be nice here, Cora. Move on, I have."

"We will see about that."

"Was that a threat? Are you threatening the Alpha's second?" Jenkins stood up and glared at the woman. The entire bar was so silent you could hear a pin drop.

Jenkins was a flirt and a bit of an asshole, but he was one hell of a guard.

"No, I was informing him that his decision was the wrong one. I am his mate and I can prove it."

"This should be good," Cole laughed.

"I'm pregnant," she yelled and Nico knew it was a lie.

"Whose child is it because you and I were never together?" Thank god for small favors. If he had slept with her, which he admittedly almost did twice, he might be on the hook for a lifetime of hell.

"We were together on Memorial day."

"We most definitely have never slept together, not even once. I remember Memorial day. I remember you were trashed. I also remember you leaving and I was not with you. God knows where you went or who you went with, but it wasn't me," Nico snapped. "If you are going to accuse someone of fathering a child… a child I doubt you are even carrying, then make sure you actually slept with them."

"They have DNA tests now that can tell who your real baby's Daddy is," Susanne, another of the guards who was on the other side having dinner, called.

"No one asked you," Cora raged.

"I'm not sure if or why you would lie about that. Go to the Clinic and make sure you're even pregnant, then we can start to look for whoever the father is."

"We were together. I remember," she wasn't yelling anymore.

"You were probably drunk. Lay off the T8."

T8 was the only concoction that could get a Shifter drunk. Alcohol gave a slight buzz that lasted minutes before the Shifter metabolism burned it off. T8 acted like alcohol did in humans. Too much was never a good idea.

"Sir, I am making an official report that this woman threatened the Alpha's second," Jenkins was standing at attention.

"I was a witness," Cole stood.

"As was I," Jett stood.

"Sit down, Boys," Nico smiled. "Cora, a formal report means that you could be considered for banishment. Do we really need to go there?"

"No, we don't. You are not worth it."

"Probably not," Nico smiled as the woman stormed out.

"That one is not right in the head. You don't really think she's pregnant?" Cole asked

"I didn't scent a change. A woman's scent changes when she is carrying young," Jett said as if it was normal for an unmated male to know that.

"Jett?" Nico looked at the guard.

"I have sisters. All of them have kids," Jett explained.

"I was worried for a second," Jenkins laughed.

"So was I. Nico, you really need to watch that one," Cole added.

"I can assure you that if she is pregnant, it isn't mine. Emerald warned me about her in particular. She calls the Pack house all the time."

"Emerald, now there's a woman of substance. Ten Cora's don't measure up to one of her," Jett declared.

"Is there something you want to share?" Nico asked, wondering how close Jett was to the Alpha's assistant.

"I wish. I'm just saying she's a Human single mother living alone in a Wolf Shifter pack. I heard the former Alpha's mate, god rest their souls, that she just walked right up to the place Emerald inherited and explained that her house was part of the Pack's territory and then shifted right there to prove what she said."

"I heard Gwen called Ellery human," Cole smiled.

"She's three. She doesn't know the difference. We refer to the women at Blythe's as human. She is just repeating what she's heard. It's nice having a kid around the Pack house. I hope that Alice and Blake have one soon."

"Because you don't want to be Alpha?"

"There is that. I was hoping more because they are great people and will make wonderful parents. Then, I'd have two little ones to play with."

"Or you could find your mate and have your own."

"That's what I was doing, but I think I've been going about it all wrong. I'm hoping my mate finds me."

Nico shook his head, thinking about the scene that Cora had made and how Blake would not be happy. Alice would scold him and Emerald would say she told him so. They all had told him that mating multiple people at once was not wise. His defense was that he wasn't really dating at all. It was his own damn fault that he now, evidently, had a possible stalking situation on his hands.

3

Emerald was surprised when only one woman and two phone calls came into the Pack house looking for Nico. None of those was from Cora.

She had heard from Jett that Cora had made a scene at the Den and she was aware that Blake and Alice had a meeting scheduled that day about the incident.

"Good morning, Beautiful," Jett said as he and Susanne entered the Pack house.

"Good morning, are you two here for the meeting with Blake?"

"Yes, and Jett would like to take you to dinner. I'm here for moral support," Susanne grinned.

"His moral support or mine?" Emerald asked.

"Either," Susanne shrugged.

"We don't have to call it a date. I know you are not my mate, but I do like your company. We discussed it and you need to get out."

"You discussed it with who?" Emerald was slightly offended.

"Cole, Susanne, and I discussed that you needed a night out. When was the last time you just cut loose and had fun?"

"What year is it?"

"Exactly, I would like to take you to dinner, no strings attached."

"Why you?"

"Jett and Cole thought that you might want a Male escort," Susanne smiled.

"I'm confused. Is this a Shifter thing? Why would I need a Male escort to have dinner? Is it because I'm human?"

"There are several men interested in you around here. You have to know that?" Susanne smiled.

"I have noticed that many of the men that come in here make sure to touch me. I am getting used to the not-so-subtle ways some men make contact. Alice explained that it was mostly innocent, to gauge whether I'm their mate or not."

"It's more than that. Men like Physical contact, like now. Jett, stop petting her."

"I was encouraging her to take our dinner offer."

"As much as I'd like to say yes to dinner out, Susanne. You know I have Gwen to think about."

"I can watch her," a familiar voice startled her.

"You would babysit so I could go to dinner?" Emerald asked Nico as he strolled into the room.

"Susanne's right. You deserve a night out, go."

"Is six tomorrow night good?" Susanne winked.

"Gwen needs to be in bed at seven," Emerald looked to Nico.

"I will be at your place at five," Nico grinned.

"You're sure?"

"Yes, go have fun."

"Alright then, I'd love to have dinner," Emerald shrugged.

She liked Jett but not like that. She was oddly offended that Nico didn't object to her going out. In the back of her mind, she wanted him to care for her as much as he cared for her daughter. She wanted him to see her as a woman.

Nico had grown on her over the weeks she had worked there. The man had hit on her the second she was hired and she turned him down flat. Now, she knew him better and, other than dating far too many women, some who had a screw loose, he was a good guy. One day, he would settle down. It was stupid for her to wish that might be with her.

"The Den at six. Do you need a ride there?" Jett grinned.

"She has a car, Jett. She will meet you there, Susanne," Nico nodded.

Emerald realized that he thought she was having dinner with Susanne, not Jett. She was about to say something when Susanne answered him.

"Six it is." The woman's smirk said she was up to something. Emerald didn't know what.

Jett and Susanne went to see Blake, along with Nico. Emerald hadn't gotten the whole story, but apparently, Cora had made a scene. It had to have been one hell of a scene to require a meeting with the Alpha.

"Mommy, no wed," Gwen looked up from her coloring book, surrounded by an explosion of crayons.

"Your Red crayon is right here," Emerald picked up the crayon and the top half flopped to the side. Only the paper wrapper was holding it together.

"Broke."

"Yes, but look, now you have two little reds." Emerald took the paper wrapper off and presented Gwen with the two pieces.

Emerald loved that the Alpha and Alice allowed Gwen to come to the Pack house with her. The weird mansion in the middle of nowhere that she had inherited had been a godsend.

While taking time off from a job she hated to spend time with her newborn, she had decided to make a life change. The tiny City apartment was no place for a little girl to grow up.

A formal letter from a Law firm informed her that she was the last living relative of a man she had only heard rumors about when her mother was alive. Her Great Uncle, or something like that, had been a wealthy recluse that dropped off the radar of the family nearly eighty years ago.

Emerald had the answers her mother would have loved but wouldn't have believed. The man had found love with a Shifter woman. He had made a home here, built a mansion in the forest, and lived to the ripe old age of one hundred and ten.

It had been the sign she needed.

Gwen's father, or Sperm donor, wanted nothing to do with Emerald the second she told him she was expecting. That too was a sign. She would have been miserable with a man she hardly knew. He would have resented Gwen.

The mansion had its drawbacks.

The Alpha was still helping her renovate and update portions of the building and grounds. She was living in a Wolf Shifter town as a human. That wasn't half as scary as it sounds, and she got to bring her daughter to work.

Worries about how Gwen would do in school eventually and, as a teen, Gwen dating shifters who were very *'hands on'*, were worries for another day.

Glancing down at Gwen, who was now breaking all of her crayons in half so she would have two of each, Emerald smiled.

"Mr. Nico is going to watch you tomorrow night at our house. Does that sound good?" she asked Gwen.

"I like Mr. Nico."

"I know you do." Emerald thanked the fates, or whoever was in charge, that Nico was in Gwen's like.

Gwen saw him as a surrogate Father figure. Emerald wasn't going to ever tell him that. It might scare him away. When the man finally found his mate, she might not like someone else's kid in the mix, another worry for another day. Emerald had a pile of worries like any other single Human mother living in a Wolf Shifter pack. She was taking each day as it came. Tomorrow night, she would go out for the first time since Gwen was born and leave her daughter with a man, who she was starting to wish was hers.

4

"Where is he?" Cora yelled, throwing the door open so hard it hit the wall.

"Good morning, Cora. I assume you're talking about Nico. He is in a meeting. Can I take a message?" Emerald grinned. The meeting was about Cora.

"Here is the message," Cora slammed a Home Pregnancy test onto her desk.

"You have to be joking?" Emerald was sure that Nico had told Blake that he had never gone as far as sleeping with Cora.

"This isn't a joke. This proves he is my mate. Shifters don't just get knocked up by random men." The woman had the nerve to glance at Gwen.

"So, you are saying this test proves you are pregnant?"

"Duh."

"Duh," Gwen repeated then laughed.

"That's not nice, Gwen. Cora, even if this is a real positive test, I doubt it's Nico's."

"I'm done listing to a stupid human. Just tell him I'm here."

"Gladly." Emerald was not offended by the woman's words. She was looking forward to the entertainment to come.

When Blake answered, she smiled at Cora. "Sir, one of the Pack women, Cora, is here demanding to see Nico."

"He is with the Alpha?" Cora went wide-eyed.

"Yes, Sir, I'll make sure she does," Emerald sighed. "They will all be right out."

"I didn't know he was in a meeting with the Alpha. You should have told me that."

"You didn't ask," Emerald grinned.

The Home Pregnancy test sat on the edge of her desk and clearly showed a positive result. Emerald trusted that Nico hadn't lied about sleeping with her, since he was so forthcoming about the women he did sleep with. Hopefully, Cora had borrowed someone else's test, because the thought of this woman being a mother to some poor child made Emerald cringe.

"Mr. Nico, the bad lady called Mommy U-man and hit her desk with a stick," Gwen called, seeing a group of five very angry looking shifters coming down the hall. Nico scooped the three-year-old up, then looked for answers.

"She did?" Nico looked up at Emerald and she just pointed to the Waiting area.

"It is a Home Pregnancy stick."

"Good god, Cora, explain," Nico roared as he put Gwen down.

"I told you I was your mate." Emerald couldn't help but notice that she had toned it down, now that the Alpha was there.

"Cora, you can't just tell someone you are their mate," Blake looked back at Nico.

"I was never intimate with this woman," he said clearly. "If she's pregnant, then it isn't mine."

"You would deny your own child?" Cora was not a very good actress.

"That's enough," Alice stepped in. "Cora, if this Pregnancy test is actually yours, it's not proof of who the father is or that you are actually pregnant. We are going to the Clinic. You will take another test, give blood and saliva for a DNA test. Nico, I will need you to do the DNA test as well. If this is Nico's, the tests will show it conclusively."

"You can have whatever you need to prove I didn't sleep with this woman."

"Duh," Gwen said from beside him with her hand on her hip. Emerald lost it and started laughing.

"What's so funny, Bitch?" Cora growled.

"That's it, out ide. We are all going to the Clinic now. That's an order."

"But Alpha?"

"Don't '*but Alpha*' me. You are clearly lying about something. I hope to god the whole pregnancy is a lie. If Nico says it isn't his, then I trust my second. You have insulted my assistant, used foul language in front of a child, and I heard all about the scene you caused at the Den."

"He wasn't answering my calls."

"When the test comes back, proving this is all in your head, I don't ever want to see you again here or anywhere else."

"I believe that Jenkins suggested banishment. You did use threatening language. Both Jett and Susanne confirmed it," Alice added.

"I was just trying to get him to listen."

"He heard you. Let's go see about that Blood test. Alice, how long will it take to prove?"

"If she isn't pregnant, less than a day. If she is, I'll drive the samples to Zeke in the Shadow pack myself and wait for the result."

"I don't like needles."

"Too bad, march," Blake pointed to the door.

"Take this nasty pee stick with you," Emerald pointed to the test.

"I could test the test to see if it is even hers," Alice said and Cora looked a little green. Emerald wasn't sure that was even possible, but the expression on Cora's face was priceless.

Blake followed Alice and Cora out, while Nico guided Gwen back to her play area. "What happened here?" he said crouching down.

"I gots two now."

"Yes, you do," he looked up at Emerald, who shrugged.

"She broke one and cried. I told her that now they were two. The result is two of each."

"Clever girl, Emerald, I really didn't sleep with that woman."

"I'm hoping she's not actually pregnant at all, that poor baby."

"I'm worried that she might actually believe she is pregnant with your child, Sir. She's not all there," Susanne added.

"We will cross that bridge. Emerald, I'll hopefully be back soon. If any calls or emails come in for Blake, you can transfer them to the Clinic."

"And if they are calling for you?" Emerald smiled.

"Tell them I'm joining a monastery. Better yet, tell them I met my mate."

"Sir, announcing that you found a mate would be a mistake," Susanne told him.

"Why would that be a mistake? They would leave me alone if they thought I was taken."

"Yes, they would, but after last night, they would also assume you mean Cora."

"I'm obviously not thinking straight. I'll be at the Clinic, Emerald, just hold my calls."

5

The following day was beautiful, so Emerald decided to just walk the two miles to work. Gwen made it two thirds of the way to the Pack house before deciding she needed to be carried.

"No car today?" Alice asked, seeing them come up the street.

"It's really not that far and it was so nice out. I have a stroller at home and didn't think to bring it."

"I can give you a ride home later if you wish. I heard you have a date."

"It's sort of a date, I guess. Jett is taking me to dinner. I think Susanne put him up to it."

"And Nico is babysitting?"

"Yes, he volunteered when he heard Susanne talking about it. I don't think he knows I'm going with Jett."

"He thinks you are going with Susanne," Alice assumed.

"Yes, I don't know why I didn't correct his assumption. I'm a grown woman and clearly single. It's no secret."

"Has Nico ever asked you out on a date?"

"Nico doesn't date Alice. He hooks up with women for a night or two. With all the phone calls that come in, I have a very clear picture of his love life."

"He told Blake he was cutting back."

"After the Cora thing, he should just stop dating altogether."

"If the Universe wants him to find a mate, it will find a way. I agree with you that he has been a little too cavalier with women's hearts."

"Did the test come back?"

"I gave her another home test. It was negative. The Blood test should come back today. If it's negative, the DNA test will not be necessary."

"I fear for any child that woman has."

"I believe Nico when he says it is not his."

"So do I, If I didn't trust him, I wouldn't have him babysit."

"You should tell him it's Jett that you are meeting and not Susanne."

"I don't know what difference it makes. I'm not Jett's mate. We are going as friends. Just because he's male shouldn't matter."

"It might. Nico is fond of you. He seems protective of you."

"He is fond of Gwen and protective of me by association. I told him I wasn't about to be another notch in his bedpost."

"So, he did ask you out?"

"He suggested that I might be his mate." Before Alice could get excited, she added, "He was joking. He said because I cared about his drama, that I might be his. Then, he offered to rock my world." Emerald glanced at Gwen to make sure she was not paying attention to the conversation.

"What did you say to that?"

"I agreed that he could rock my world. It's been over three years since I was with a man and that was nothing to write home about. I declined Nico's offer. I don't share. I had one short-term affair and got pregnant. The fact that he wanted nothing to do with me after that was a blessing."

"Nico would settle down with a mate."

"I'm not looking forward to that."

"You don't want Nico to find a mate or you don't want to be that mate?"

"If I was his, which I'm pretty sure I'm not, I guess I'd prefer that. It's Gwen and her connection to him that I hope never goes away. I already feel guilty she doesn't have a Dad. I'm not stupid enough to just find the next guy that will have me to give her a Dad. Nico is her Male Role model. He is so good with her. If he finds his mate and they have kids, what happens with Gwen?"

"Unless, that mate is you."

"Right," Emerald rolled her eyes.

"Emerald, how many women do you think he says might be his mate?"

"I don't know what he tells his women."

"I can guarantee you are the only one he's brought up the word mate with."

"Because I'm human?"

"Because he sees you as the perfect woman. Maybe, you are what he is looking for?"

"Stop matchmaking. Is this a service you provide to all of your patients? Is that why two of the Human women at the Bed and Breakfast are now mated to Shifter men?"

"I had nothing to do with Jazz. I might have pushed Ellery just a little."

"I am not looking for a mate, Alice. I'm going on my first date in nearly four years with a man who isn't my mate and I'm not his. We are friends."

"So, why didn't you correct Nico when he assumed it was Susanne you were going with?"

"I don't know. I thought he might be upset and not sit for Gwen."

"Why would he be upset, Emerald?" Alice grinned.

"End of conversation, I have work to do. I'm leaving early today to make sure Gwen is settled before Nico arrives."

"I don't mean to push," Alice started to apologize.

"Yes, you do. You want everyone to be as happy as you are with Blake. I watched you two figure things out. I honestly hope to have that one day, even though I'm human. I just can't let that hope interfere with my reality. I'm a single mother of a three-year-old and, before you say it, Nico being the perfect Father figure to Gwen wouldn't be enough. I deserve more and he's looking for his true mate, not a single Mom who is human."

"You are only assuming you are not his mate, am I right?"

"I have not hugged him or jumped him. I haven't pet him like the men tend to do to me, so, no, I can't be sure. I can be sure I don't want to be part of the man's stable."

"I don't think you would be."

"Alright, are we finally done here? Can I get to work?"

"Yes, of course," Alice smiled, "you know that I mean well."

"I know you do. Alice, I'm happy the way I am. Maybe, when Gwen is in college, I will look for someone to keep me company."

"You don't want more children?"

"I do want more eventually. I have my hands full at the moment."

"Yes, you do," Alice glanced at Gwen's play area. The wall and the floor were covered with blue paint.

"I guess Nico bought her more blue paint," Emerald sighed

"Tell him to clean it," Alice laughed.

"I just might do that."

By Lynn Leite

6

Emerald was nearly done for the day when Alice gestured to her to come into the Living room.

"Shush," Alice said as she put a finger to her lips.

The sight Emerald found nearly made her cry.

Gwen, tucked under Nico's arm, was watching something on Disney and Nico was sound asleep. The feeling in her chest was overwhelming. People needed to stop even suggesting that Nico was hers. As good as he was with her daughter, she didn't want a man just to give her daughter a father. She wanted a mate, a husband who loved her and her daughter.

It hit her like a two-ton truck. She was in love with the man now snoring next to her daughter. The feeling had nothing to do with Gwen; well, maybe a little to do with Gwen. It was Emerald that had fallen as well as Gwen. Nico was a playboy with a stalker who joked more than he was serious, but he was strong and kind, he always treated Emerald with respect, and he was one hell of a Father figure.

"Emerald," Alice looked concerned.

"Yes," she whispered as Alice pulled her away from the loving scene.

"You were crying."

"I got a little choked up seeing Gwen cuddled next to someone that wasn't me."

"You got choked up because it was Nico."

"Don't start that again."

"Mommy, Mr. Nico seeping," Gwen came toddling in after them

"Yes, Gwen I saw that."

"He tired," Gwen nodded and went back to her play area.

Nico was tired and the reason that he might not have gotten much sleep was something Emerald didn't want to think about. Late night with some woman, maybe even more than one, was probably the main reason. Her brain went there, despite her heart not wanting to imagine what Nico did with his evenings. Tonight, he was watching Gwen for at least part of the evening.

Taking a deep breath, Emerald forced herself to think of something other than Nico's love life. That was hard to do since she had already intercepted one phone call that day from a woman saying she hadn't heard from him in a while. One phone call was nothing compared to what he used to get. Perhaps, he was cutting back to search for a real connection. That thought brought her full circle back to realizing she had genuine feelings for the man.

"Alice, we are going to get going."

"Right, you have a big date tonight."

"I have a dinner engagement," Emerald smiled.

"I will make sure that Nico wakes up in time to babysit."

"Thank you." Emerald gathered Gwen's things and took her hand.

"I need say bye Mr. Nico."

"Mr. Nico will be at our house in a few hours. You will see him then," Emerald assured her as they walked out the door.

Two hours later, Nico was in her house, picking another movie to watch with Gwen, while they both ate Mac and Cheese on the couch.

"My mommy would never let me eat on the couch," Nico whispered to Gwen

"Why?" Gwen asked as Nico and she chatted.

"Because I dropped a lot and it made a mess."

"I like mess," Gwen smiled up at him.

"I know. I saw the blue paint I bought was all over the entry hall."

"It was pretty," Gwen beamed.

"Yes, it was," Nico grinned.

Emerald had to turn away before she did something stupid like hug Nico. Normally, hugging would be a natural thing to do to a man who was so kind to her daughter. With shifters, hugging could mean a lot more. At this point, she was still avoiding the man's touch, not because he might think she was his mate. Now, it was because she feared he *wouldn't* think so.

"Are you ready?" Nico's question startled her.

She had to get her head on straight. She was having dinner with a man. She shouldn't be thinking about another man. She wasn't Jett's mate. He had made that clear. Being human, she wasn't sure she even understood how a shifter knew so definitively when they met the right one.

"Yes, I won't be late," Emerald said, gathering her keys.

"No rush, I don't have any other plans."

"Alright, I'm off," Emerald said, making sure to let Gwen know she was leaving, not that Gwen seemed to care.

The drive to The Den was a short one. It took a few minutes for her to get up the nerve to walk in. It was a Shifter bar and she was human. She reasoned that most of the shifters in the area knew her. Jett was already there. He had texted her when he arrived. It was still the first time she was out with a man since Gwen was born.

"Hey there," Jett stood, waving as she entered the restaurant portion.

"Hi," she called back softly.

"I hope you don't mind Cole joining us."

"I don't mind at all," Emerald sighed. Jett alone was a date. Jett and Cole together were friends having dinner.

"I didn't know if you'd be uncomfortable," Cole offered as she took a seat.

"Two Pack guards as Dinner companions. Why would that make me uncomfortable? I'm not Jett's mate and I'm not yours, unless you have something to tell me," Emerald smiled.

"No, sadly you are not mine," Cole laughed."

"Then, we are just three friends having dinner. We should call Susanne."

"She's on duty," Jett explained.

"This was her idea. We should have done it on a night she could come," Emerald sighed.

"I think she was hoping you would be either mine or Jett's," Cole shrugged." I'd gladly take you as a girlfriend, but I couldn't promise forever. You seem like the forever type."

"I am the Mom type. I think most women want forever at some point. It doesn't matter if they are human or shifter. You guys are lucky. You, at least, have assurance when you meet the right woman."

"It's terrifying," Jett groaned.

"What's terrifying about instantly knowing you've found your soulmate?"

"Imagine a man you don't know comes up and, with one touch, declares you are his."

"I guess it would depend on the man," Emerald responded. "If I don't know him, I'm not sure I'd believe him."

"That's because you are human, but if you're a shifter, you have to take it seriously, because maybe they are right."

"I never really thought too much about it until recently," Cole added

"What changed?" Emerald asked.

"The Alpha found his mate. It sometimes effects a pack. Those of Mating age become more attuned or something. Ghost found a mate, then Eli. It's just a matter of time now. The Shadow Pack and the Moon Valley had a rash of matings after their Alphas took a mate."

"Sort of like when all of your girlfriends are getting married and you're wondering when it's your turn?"

"Exactly," Cole smiled, "change of subject, or maybe not. Did Alice ever get the Pregnancy result from the Queen of Crazy?"

"The Queen of Crazy?"

"If she's not pregnant by Nico and I believe him when he says he never went there, then she's a six-pack short of a dozen. How in this day and age did she think she could pull that off, even if she was pregnant?"

"She isn't pregnant. The tests were negative. I don't know if she knows that yet, but Alice got the result back just before Gwen and I left."

"Gwen is officially my favorite little person. When she said that the bad lady said a mean thing then hit your desk with a stick, I almost lost it."

"When was this?" Cole asked.

"The meeting about the scene she made at the Den. The stick was the Pregnancy test, the positive one," Jett explained.

Emerald sat back as the two men speculated who might have given the test to Cora. They discussed Cora and other crazy women who were willing to trap a man, even if that man was theirs.

"Could it be she really thinks that Nico is her mate?" Emerald asked.

"Sometimes, we want to believe something so much that we lose track of what's real," Jett said sadly. Emerald knew there was a story there but didn't ask.

By Lynn Leite

"The moment I found I was pregnant with Gwen, believe me, I was rooted firmly in reality."

7

Nico wandered from room to room, making a list of things that needed doing around the home. When Emerald was hired by Blake, she didn't ask for money. Nico was sure she thought she'd try the job out for a couple of days then back out. The Alpha had offered a Lawn service and groundskeeper, along with any work that needed doing to keep the place livable and safe enough for a three-year-old.

Emerald stayed and so did the Alpha's deal, along with a small wage for food and such. Emerald was a proud woman. Nico had no idea if she had a savings or an inheritance before that she was living on.

Gwen was in bed her tiny room, decorated with fairies and butterflies. He had peeked into the Master bedroom where Emerald slept. Her scent was all over the home but more concentrated in that space.

As he jotted down what needed painting, what needed repairing, even just freshening up, he sensed someone outside. Rushing to the door, he opened it ready to fight.

"Good evening." Susanne's presence on the doorstep put him in a state of panic.

"Where is Emerald? Is she alright? What happened?" Nico's heart was pounding out of his chest.

"Oh, sorry, she's fine, Sir, really. She's not hurt. She is at the Den having dinner with Jett."

"With Jett?" Growling at Sussanne had been involuntary.

"Yes, with Jett, is there a problem?"

"She said she was going to dinner with you."

"No, Sir, she said she was going to dinner. I encouraged her to go and you volunteered to stay with Gwen. You never actually asked who she was going with."

"I thought she was going with you," Nico said, surprised by his own reaction.

"Yes, I see that. She's fine."

"She went on a date," Nico was mainly speaking to himself.

"Yes, I guess you could call it a date. Jett was clear that she wasn't his mate when he asked her. She needed to get out. Don't you agree?" Susanne was enjoying the many expressions crossing Nico's features.

"Why are you here?"

"I am on duty tonight, Sir. Eli asked that I warn you that Cora was not at home. Alice said to let you know she is disputing the Pregnancy test results."

"Alice is disputing them?"

"No, Cora is. She's probably out trying to get knocked up by some poor man so that she can claim it's yours. She's not right in the head. Eli thought you should know."

"Thank you. Have Ghost track her. I don't like that she's out there when Emerald is not at home."

"You think she will be after Emerald?" Susanne asked.

"No, I think your theory about her trying to get impregnated by morning is probably what's going on. Did you sense her anywhere around here?"

"Not yet, but that is the other reason I'm here. You are here. She might show up looking for you. I don't think she knows you were babysitting, but you can't be too careful."

"I don't know what she knows. Stick around the house until Ghost locates her. I can't leave. Unless you want to stay and I'll check the perimeter."

"I love Emerald and I think Gwen is cute as hell, but I don't know the first thing about kids. You stay with Gwen. I'll do a sweep."

"Thank you, Susanne."

Nico wasn't sure what was wrong with him. He trusted Jett, yet when he thought about Emerald and Jett together, he had trouble thinking straight.

He should have been concerned that Cora was not accepting the tests that Alice had done. If she was convinced that they had been together and that she was pregnant, there was no telling what extremes she would go to.

Instead of thinking of ways to solve the Cora problem, he was fixated on Emerald being out with Jett. Why hadn't she told him it was a date? He hadn't actually asked, but she might have mentioned it.

This feeling that he was feeling was bad. If he hadn't been responsible for Gwen, he would have gone to the Den. Nico was confused by his own reaction.

Picking up the phone, he called the one person that might have a clue as to why his chest was tight and his wolf was nipping at his subconscious.

"Nico, is everything alright?" Alice asked before he could speak.

"I'm not sure. Did you know Emerald was on a date?"

"Nico, you are at her house babysitting Gwen, aren't you?"

"Yes, Alice, I thought Emerald was going out with Susanne."

"No, she was going to dinner with Jett."

"Susanne was just here about Cora."

"I heard. Are you worried about Emerald? I don't think Cora knows how close you are."

"I didn't know how close we were. Alice, I'm crawling out of my skin here. "

"Because she's on a date, or is it because it's Jett?"

"Jett is a good guy. I didn't know she was having dinner with a man."

"She's allowed a life, Nico."

"Why didn't she tell me this was a date?"

"She might have assumed you already knew, Nico, or maybe, she didn't think it was really any of your business."

"I'm having a hard time here, Alice."

"So, this is a professional call?" He could tell that Alice was smiling.

"Yes, it is. I don't know why I'm upset."

"Are you upset she didn't tell you or are you upset she is out with a man?"

"Both, I don't like that she's dating at all."

"Yet, she fields phone calls and unwanted visits from women you have slept with every day. Seems a bit unfair of you to weigh in on her love life."

"Jett isn't her mate."

"Neither are the women you sleep with."

"I get it. I'm a hypocrite. I called because, if I wasn't watching Gwen, I would be at the Den ruining her date."

"Because you like her for yourself?"

"I don't know. That's why I'm calling you."

"I'm no psychic, Nico. I can't tell you what you are feeling or thinking. You need to decide why you are so upset."

"She deserves better."

"Better than Jett or better than you?"

"I'd know if she was my mate, wouldn't I?"

"Not necessarily, when was the last time you touched her?"

"Never."

"In that case, my recommendation would be to touch her."

"Your Professional recommendation as a therapist is that I ignore her request, that I not shake hands?"

"That was months ago and in response to you hitting on her pretty blatantly."

"She said she didn't want to be another notch on my bedpost."

"She told me," Alice said softly.

"What else did she tell you?"

"She told me that you suggested that she might be your mate. She said that she thought you were kidding around, but maybe subconsciously, you were telling the truth."

"What do you suggest I do now?"

"I'd say figuring out if she is your mate would be a good start."

"And if she isn't?"

"Then, butt out of her love life."

8

It was not too late when Emerald arrived home. The lights in the Living room silhouetted Nico pacing back and forth. That worried her.

Parking her car, she rushed to make sure everything was alright with Gwen. She had left her daughter with Nico many times but never this long or at night.

"Nico, I'm home," she called thinking for a second about how that sounded.

"How was your date?" There was so much venom in his tone, she felt it like a slap.

"Are you angry? It isn't that late. You could have called and asked that I come home if you had plans."

"I didn't have plans. I spoke to Susanne."

"Why?"

"Because she came here. She was on duty tonight."

"I know that."

"You told me you were going to dinner with Susanne."

"Back up, I said no such thing. I was talking to Susanne and Jett about getting out. Jett asked me to dinner and Susanne was encouraging me when you came in and volunteered to watch Gwen."

"I volunteered to watch Gwen so you could go to dinner with Susanne."

"I don't see the difference."

"He is an unmated male."

"Oh really? I hadn't noticed. For your information, I had dinner with two unmated males, not just one. I assumed that you had overheard the entire conversation with your Super-Shifter hearing."

"Who was the other male?"

"That is not your business. Thank you for watching Gwen, but it's time for you to go."

"I want to know who you were out with," Nico said slowly.

"I want a million dollars to fall from the sky. I guess we will both be disappointed."

"Emerald, you don't understand."

"You are right. I don't understand. I had a nice evening and you basically attack me when I come home. I didn't do anything wrong, so I don't know why you're acting like I committed a crime."

"I don't like the idea of you dating."

"You have made that perfectly clear. I will ask Susanne or Alice to watch Gwen, if and when I go out again. You have at least five women you are seeing and sleeping with, but I can't go out with two male friends without you judging me. Go home, Nico."

"I wasn't judging."

"Funny, it sure seemed like it. Is it because I'm human? Is that the problem? God forbid someone was interested in the poor, single Human mother, or was it Gwen you were worried about? I can assure you I would make sure a man was going to stick around long term before introducing *my* daughter to him."

"I think, maybe, I'm your mate," he yelled.

"You have got to be kidding."

"I'm not kidding. I'm not judging. I just can't handle you dating is all."

"But it's okay for you to screw every woman in the pack. Go home, Nico. I'm tired and I don't want to argue."

"Humor me and take my hand," Nico extended his arm to reach for her.

"Then what?" Emerald asked, crossing her arms against her chest.

"Then, we will know."

"Then, you will know. I'm human, remember? It doesn't always work for humans. Maybe, I don't want a mate at all."

"Are you scared to touch me?"

"Yes."

"Is that because you want me or because you don't?"

"I want a man who trusts me, who respects me, who loves me for me, not some tingling in his extremities because I took his hand. I want something real."

"I am real."

"You are a wonderful man. You are so good with Gwen. You are kind and strong. You also have half the pack hoping you are their mate, one who went as far as telling you they were pregnant."

"If you are mine, then all of those women don't matter."

"To you they don't, but to them, you still might mean something. To me, they would still seem like competition. I don't understand mating or how some shifters just know when they found the one. I don't trust it."

"So, why not take my hand?"

"Because I don't know how I will feel if you're right, and I don't want to know how I would feel if you are wrong."

"You like the idea. I can tell," Nico smirked.

"Go home, Nico."

"I will go home, but this discussion isn't over."

Nico took a step toward her. She held her ground, not because she was being stubborn, but because she wanted him to make the first move.

"Nico!" she warned when he took another step.

"Yes, Emerald."

"I'm scared."

"I know." He looked into her eyes for permission, then reached out to her, pulling her in and kissing her.

Emeralds hands pressed against Nico's chest as he kissed her. She had meant to push him away, but instead, she just rested them there, feeling the electric current that was pulsing between them. He was a live wire and she couldn't let go, despite knowing she should.

"Still scared," Nico asked, holding her against his chest.

"Terrified," she sighed.

"I'm going to go now."

"Alright." Emerald wanted to ask him to stay. Was what she felt a Mating pull or was it just Nico? For all she knew, that's why the women kept coming back for more.

"Are we good? I didn't push too hard, did I?"

"We are good."

He still hadn't said that she was his mate or if he had been wrong. Emerald wasn't about to ask. She had asked one other man for some sort of commitment too early in a relationship and he had run for the hills. Losing Gwen's father was no loss, since Gwen never met the man. If Nico walked or pulled away because they weren't meant to be, then Gwen would suffer. Emerald would suffer as well.

"I'm going to check on Gwen," Emerald said shyly.

As soon as Nico left, Emerald collapsed into a chair. Was that the first kiss or the last? He had rocked her world as promised and she still had all of her clothes on. He hadn't mentioned what he felt, if anything. For her, the kiss had opened up more questions than answers.

9

"Where is Emerald?" Nico asked Alice.

"At home, I assume. It's Saturday. She doesn't normally come in on Saturdays."

"That's right." Nico felt a little bit calmer.

"You could drive over there to see her."

"I kissed her," he blurted.

"And?"

"She is my mate."

"Then, why are you here talking to me? Did she kick you out?"

"She asked me to go a few times before I kissed her. I messed up and was acting jealous. She didn't like it."

"I can't blame her. You had no claim on her and, even if you did, you should trust her. What did she say when you told her how you felt?"

"I... I..."

"Nico, you did tell her that you felt she was yours after you kissed her?"

"I assumed it was obvious."

"You kissed her then left without telling her that you thought she was your future mate?"

"I told her before that I thought she was mine."

"You didn't follow up with an '*I told you so* or *see I was right*'? You didn't ask her what she felt, if anything?"

"No."

"You are an idiot."

"She felt it. I know she did."

"That's even worse, Nico. She felt it and you didn't acknowledge that you did. Right about now, she's second-guessing everything. She's human. Even if she was shifter, you'd have to let her know what you felt."

"Tell Blake I went to see Emerald."

"Will do," Alice smiled as Nico ran from the building.

The Manor house that Emerald had inherited was quiet when he got there. Taking out his cell phone, he called rather than crash in the front door. He wasn't sure that he would be welcomed at this point.

"Hello," Emerald answered.

"Where the hell are you?"

"Hello, Nico, nice of you to call. Be sure to call again when you find your manners," she said and hung up.

Nico was stunned. He had heard that Emerald put more than one Pack member in their place, but he had never witnessed it firsthand. Working for Blake as an assistant, she had to handle a number of unwanted visitors to the Pack house, starting with Danielle, who was after Blake before he mated Alice. She had never been that way with him. They bantered, they joked, but just now, she had shut him down.

Dialing again, he waited.

"Hello."

"I'm sorry I was rude. I am at your house and you are not here. I got worried."

"That's better. Gwen woke with a fever. We are at the doctors."

"Why didn't you call?"

"Nico, why would I call you because my daughter was sick? I didn't even call Alice. Gwen is the H-word and I took her to a H-Doctor at the hospital in town."

"Is she okay?"

"We are waiting to be seen. Fevers are common in kids. I just wanted to be sure. I'll call when we are back home."

"I messed up last night. I should have told you what I felt."

"Yes, you should have. I can't do this right now. I will call you later."

Nico knew better than to call Emerald back after she hung up on him for a second time. She was worried about Gwen.

Nico couldn't sit still and wait. He stopped by the homes by the lake to see Ghost and check on where Cora had ended up. It was a good distraction.

"You have a stalker," Ghost said calmly.

"I know that. That was the reason for you to track her. Where was she?"

"All over the place, she was at your place behind the back gate of the Pack house. Her scent was strong, so I imagine she was there a while. Then, she went for a run, circling back to the Den."

"Emerald was at the Den. Did she go in?"

"Not that I could tell, I asked around and no one had seen her."

"I assume you found her."

"She left the Blue Rock Pack land for a while then re-entered the wards on the North side. I caught up with her on the old fork road."

"Doing what?"

"Walking like she didn't have a care in the world. I told her to go home."

"And did she?"

"Yes, I didn't like the look on her face. She's up to something."

"Susanne thought she might have been hooking up with someone, hoping to get pregnant so that she could claim it's mine. She is disputing the tests that Alice made her take."

"She is slightly off her rocker. Does Blake know?"

"He is considering banishment if she doesn't get her act together. I never even slept with the woman and she's gone insane."

"Dating multiple women is dangerous business."

"I know that now. I have a stalker, a few others that are hanging on, and a mate that probably doesn't believe she's mine."

"A mate, Nico?"

"Yes, Emerald."

"Congratulations, that explains your attachment to the little one."

"It could have something to do with it. Don't congratulate me until I fix the mess I made."

"What mess?" Jazz, Ghost's mate came out from their home. "What did you do?"

"You used to be human. Can I ask you something?"

"Sure."

"When you and Ghost first got together…"

"Are we talking sex or just making out?"

"Making out," Nico smiled at the bluntness of this woman.

"Go on."

"Did you know he was yours? Could you tell he was different from other men you'd kissed?"

"Yes, I didn't know how or why, since at that point, I still had no clue you were all shifters, but I knew. Why do you ask?"

"I kissed Emerald."

"And?"

"Then, I left."

"Ouch, you just left. Didn't you say anything to her?"

"She had asked me to leave before I kissed her. I told her I'd see her today and she knew before I kissed her that I thought she was mine. I told her. I messed up by not assuring her that I was right after I kissed her."

"Then, why are you here?"

"She took Gwen to the Doctor's. I was checking on Cora."

"The not pregnant one."

"She wasn't pregnant two days ago. Who knows what she did since then?"

"Does she know you found a mate? That might make her back off."

"No, you and Ghost know. Alice knows, which means Blake already knows."

"But Emerald doesn't," Jazz reminded.

"I am going to fix that as soon as they are back."

"It's hard to understand the intensity of the feelings, Nico, even though she knows shifters exist and knows there's some weird instinct that tells you all when you have met your life partner. It's hard for a human to wrap their head around it, even if they feel it. She might need a lot of assurance and time. I just went for it. She has Gwen to consider."

"I love Gwen like she's my own."

"Then, I suggest you make sure Emerald knows you love her for more than just her kid."

"She wouldn't think that."

"Human woman aren't always rational thinkers," Jazz offered.

"Neither are Shifter women. Ghost, thank you for tracking Cora."

By Lynn Leite

"Anytime."

10

Emerald was exhausted. The Emergency room was backed up and, by the time they saw someone, Gwen was already feeling better. The Doctor diagnosed her with an Ear infection. An antibiotic and a pain med later, Gwen wanted burgers for dinner. She pronounced it "boogers", but Emerald was fluent in Gwen speak.

"Mr. Nico is coming?" Gwen asked as Emerald tucked her in.

"No, Gwen, that was last night. Tonight, it's just us again."

Thinking about Mr. Nico was something Emerald had tried and failed to avoid for most of the day.

"He singed a song."

"He did?"

"The bunny song, foo foo."

"I don't know that one."

Gwen either butchered the song or it was about a rabbit that hit people and got in trouble. Emerald was going to have to ask Nico. She needed to call Nico and had been avoiding it.

"Go to sleep, Gwen, feel better."

"Feel better," she mimicked and snuggled down into her pillow.

"Are you home? Is she alright?" Nico asked without saying hello. He had been staring at his phone, willing it to ring for hours now.

"She has a little Ear infection. She will be fine. It just took a while to see the Doctor. I'm going to have to find a good pediatrician in the area. The Emergency room was full of emergencies."

"I need to tell you something. Can I come over?"

"Nico, it's late and I didn't get much sleep last night."

"Was that because of me?"

"Partially, yes, it was because of you and because Gwen woke up with a fever."

"I would really like to discuss what comes next for us."

"Is there an us Nico? I spent half the night second guessing what happened. You kissed me. It confused the hell out of me."

"As far as I'm concerned, there is only us. That kiss was the first of many. I know deep down in my soul that you were meant to be mine. What I need to know is how you felt, how you feel now about me, about us?"

"I feel like I would like very much to be the last notch on your bed post. I never thought that one kiss could answer so many questions. When you didn't say anything, I worried that was just what kissing you felt like for everyone. Then, I thought about all of the women after you, crazy Cora included."

"The women are all shifters. They already know it was temporary, a fling, and not exclusive. Except for Cora that is."

"I'm not sure that's helping. I am going to need assurance, Nico. I watched Blake and Alice, then Jazz and ghost, even Eli and Ellery fall for this Mating thing. Seeing it happen and experiencing it are two different things."

"Trust your heart, Emerald. I am."

"If it was just me, I'd already have you here. It's not just me. I have Gwen to think about. Are you ready to be a Dad, because we come as a package deal?"

"I love that little girl of yours."

"I know, but part time sitter is different from full time father, Nico. If I say yes to *us*, I need to make sure it's the right thing to do for all three of us."

"Gwen should come first. We can go slow, get her used to the idea of me being around, of me being with you. I'm sending a few people there tomorrow, with your permission of course."

"For what?"

"The sink upstairs leaks. The boards in the hall squeak. The third step in the back stairwell is loose. The last bedroom on the right needs a coat of paint. You need a dishwasher that actually works, and that's only the first things on my list."

"You made a list?"

"Yes, Emerald, I might not have figured out that you were my mate just yet, but I did know I cared deeply for you and your daughter."

"Now, I feel like I should have let you come over."

"If I came over now, I'd be staying and I'm not sure your ready for that. Matings are forever, Emerald."

"I know that, Nico."

"I've decided to give you time to get used to the idea."

"Oh, you have, have you?' Emerald smiled.

"It was Jazz that suggested I might have needed to be clearer about what I felt and where I hoped to end up."

"She was right. I didn't know if you still thought I might be your mate or not?"

"I no longer think you might be. I'm sure you are. We have forever. What's a night or two?"

"I don't recall saying yes. In fact, I don't recall being asked."

"Emerald, I would like very much to take you as my soulmate, my true mate, my wife, whatever you a want to call it. If you say yes, we should discuss a few important things, but please say yes?"

"What important things? Do you mean Gwen or this house?"

"The house is yours. I don't care where we live. Uprooting Gwen to the Pack house doesn't sound practical, but you can decide. What I meant was my bite."

"Oh, that is something to think about."

"Gwen is human for now."

"What does *for now* mean?"

"Emerald, think about it, she lives in a Shifter pack. She will grow up with shifters. The likely hood of her mate being a shifter is pretty good."

"I thought, for a second, that you were suggesting turning her," Emerald sighed in relief.

"No, that would have to be her choice when she is of age. If it was to be done at all."

"Aren't there rules against that?"

"There are always exceptions. I was talking about you. You can remain human or not. It is just an option."

"I will think about it. Matings are mainly physical, right?"

"A Physical joining is a big part of it, yes, an exchange of fluids, to be technical. I don't have to bite you."

'I'll get back to you."

"You still haven't said yes, Emerald. Did you feel it? Will you accept my claim?"

"Yes, Nico, I felt it. I will accept your claim, provided you lose the harem."

"They are already gone. I called them all this morning and told them I found my mate."

"Even Cora?"

"No, I want nothing to do with that woman. I already made that clear."

"Good, I will see you in the morning."

"I'll be there before the crews show up."

"You are sending crews for a few repairs."

"I might have gotten carried away."

11

Seeing Nico pull up to her place at the crack of dawn made Emerald's stomach do flips. Talking about mating and forever on the phone was one thing. Seeing the expression on his face confirming he was hers was another thing altogether.

"Mr. Nico," Gwen squealed and ran to him.

The sight of the two of them as he lifted her into his arms meant so much more now.

"Hey," he said, leaning in to kiss Emerald's cheek. He had never done that before, of course. Gwen was bound to ask questions. Emerald looked at Gwen, expecting her to mention Mommy kissing Mr. Nico, and the three-year-old said nothing.

Nico kissing Mommy was apparently not as earth shattering as Mommy felt it was.

"Have you eaten?" Emerald asked.

"I have. Have you two had breakfast? I can run out to get you something."

"We already ate," Emerald said at the same time as Gwen said she wanted boogers.

"Boogers?" Nico looked to Emerald for help.

"She means burgers and she had one last night for dinner."

"Too many burgers are not good for little girls," Nico told Gwen

"And we don't have burgers for breakfast," Emerald added as Nico let Gwen down.

"Sing the foo, foo song?"

"Later, Gwen, can you go play? I need to talk to Mommy."

"I watch princesses?"

"Yes, but only one. Let me get her set up with today's Princess choice and we can talk. There is coffee in the kitchen," Emerald smiled as she followed Gwen into the Living room.

It took several minutes for Gwen to decide which movie was the one she wanted to watch. Emerald made sure she was fully engaged before joining Nico in the kitchen.

Wordlessly, Nico cupped her face with his hands and kissed her deeply. Her body and her mind were alive with sensation. Her knees threatened to give out at one point, but Nico repositioned and slid one arm around her back.

"Soon, Emerald," Nico sighed, trying to catch his own breath.

"Soon," she agreed.

Emerald tried to calculate in her head the average time Gwen stayed engaged when watching a Princess movie. Fifteen minutes in, she would want a drink, to go to the potty, or any number of things. It had already been nearly five.

"We have ten minutes," Emerald smiled.

"That is nowhere near enough time for what I have planned."

"What exactly do you have planned?" Emerald liked the sexy banter.

"I'd rather show you than tell you." Nico's hand was tracing Concentric circles against her back as he pressed her lower half against his.

Mary Grace, one of the rescued humans out at the B&B, had referred to Nico as tall, dark, and dangerous. He had been a trained guard before he became the Alpha's second in command. This was a whole different kind of dangerous. Her heart would shatter if he took back his claim. Her body might wither and die as well.

His arousal was a concern only because she was about to throw caution to the wind and let him claim her on the kitchen table.

A vehicle approaching the home was like a bucket of water being tossed on them.

"I need to let them in," Nico s eyes were dark and full of desire.

"I need to take a cold shower," Emerald sat down hard on one of her kitchen chairs, trying to get her bearings.

Nico laughed, kissing her quickly before heading to open the door. "Emerald?" He turned back just as he was at the door.

"Yeah?"

"We are going to be so happy."

"I'm starting to believe you, Nico."

"If you need me, just howl."

Emerald smiled as Nico went to head off the workers.

By Lynn Leite

The crew of men and some women that came to fix the things on Nico's list and more were hard at work. The noise of the saws and hammering drew Gwen away from her Princess movie. A curious three-year-old and power tools were not a great combination.

Nico brought lunch and then dinner, since some of the work was being done in the kitchen.

"How long does it take to install a dishwasher? I can cook dinner." Emerald had told Nico when he suggested they get take out from The Den for the second time that day.

"No, you aren't allowed in the kitchen."

"I'm not allowed in my own kitchen."

"Not yet, I authorized some upgrades. When they are done, you will thank me."

"I'm already thanking you. Nico, who is paying for all of this?"

"I talked to Blake and we cashed in a few favors. If I recall correctly, you were hired at a small salary and Blake promised to help with repairs and maintenance of the house."

"He did send lawn crews to tame the jungle that used to be there."

"Any cost is already taken care of. I bought all of the supplies. I assumed I would be living here after all," Nico smirked.

"It is a lot of house for just Gwen and I. I'm sure we can make room for one more," Emerald giggled.

"What about more than one?" Nico asked, pulling her in for a hug.

"You lost me, more than one?"

"I was thinking maybe a brother or sister for Gwen?"

"Oh that, I am open to the idea." Emerald knew her face was turning red. The house was full of shifters working on repairing her steps and painting. She was sure they could hear the conversation she and Nico were having.

"Good, because more than half of all True Mated couples conceive at the first joining."

"The first... oh, that is something I wasn't aware of."

"Alice and Blake are expecting. Don't tell them I told you. No one knows." Nico's voice dropped to a barely audible whisper, despite his being inches away from her ear.

"Why is it a secret?" she breathed, hoping it was below the hearing range of the workers.

"They are the Alpha couple. Their child will be the next Alpha, god willing. It is extremely rare for a Shifter woman to miscarry, but it does happen, so most wait until three months have passed to announce it. Any shifter close to Alice can sense the change. Jett says there is a scent change. I never noticed until he mentioned it." His lips were now pressed against her ear and his words were accompanied by his hot breath. Emerald had to concentrate on what he was saying rather than what his proximity was doing to her.

"Jett?"

"He apparently has a sister or two who have young. He knew Cora was not pregnant even before the test came back."

"If we have kids…"

"When we have kids," Nico smiled. His voice was back to normal, showing Emerald he was alright with being overheard. He wasn't keeping her a secret.

"Fine, when we have kids, what will they be?"

"Boy or girl would be my guess," Nico laughed.

"You know what I mean," Emerald said, glancing over to make sure Gwen was not listening.

"If you chose to remain human, then there is a one in four chance the child would be like Blythe. She's human but faster and stronger than most."

"Superhuman?"

"There would be a three out of four chance the child would be a shifter."

"If I decided to turn?"

"The children would all be Shifter. Are you considering it… turning, I mean?" Nico tried to sound neutral, but he wanted her to decide to turn for a number of reasons.

"I know shifters live longer, age slowly. I'd like to stick around to see Gwen's children have children. If you and I have kids that are shifters, then it would be hard to keep up with them as a human."

"Many Human mothers raise Shifter children in the three packs. You don't have to decide now."

"I have given it some thought."

"Tonight, tomorrow, or ten years from now, it doesn't matter. When you decide, it's your choice."

"What do you want?"

"That is a loaded question. I want you as a mate. I want you as the mother of my children. I'm not going to lie. I would like you to choose turning. I wouldn't want to live without you and humans are breakable."

By Lynn Leite

"I just need a little time. It's a big change."

"Take all the time you need."

12

A few workers were finishing up when Nico was called away.

"Duty calls," Nico smiled, kissing Emerald.

"Mr. Nico loves Mommy?" Gwen asked, looking like she was trying to solve a puzzle.

"What do you think, Gwen?" Nico asked.

"Mr. Bake kisses Miss Alice like you. They in love."

"That's right. Is it okay if I kiss Mommy?" Nico squatted down to talk to her on her level. Emerald's heart exploded. This man was so good with Gwen, he wasn't telling her that this was the way it was. He was including her in a decision they had already made.

"You love Gwen too?" she referred to herself in the Third person, making Nico smile.

"Yes, I love Gwen"

"I want kisses too."

"Grown-up's kisses are different," Nico explained.

"Grown up kisses are yucky." Gwen made a face and both of them laughed.

"Give Mr. Nico a kiss on his cheek, Gwen. He needs to go do some work."

Gwen kissed Nico's cheek and he kissed the top of her head as he stood.

"Am I coming back tonight?" he asked Emerald.

"What do you think, Gwen? Do you think we should invite Mr. Nico to live here with us?"

"Like a Daddy?"

"Yes, like a Daddy." Nico was trying to hold it together. He was the Alpha second. Alphas and Alpha seconds didn't cry. This tiny human was choking him up. He wanted very much to be her Daddy.

"Okay, you can sleep in my room," Gwen announced.

"I think Mr. Nico needs a bigger bed, Gwen," Emerald laughed.

"Okay."

"Go play your game. I'll be in in a minute." Emerald handed the toddler her phone to play on.

"I will be back as soon as I can. Blake needs me to cover the Pack house. Alice had an emergency and Blake had to go solo to the Shadow Pack Alpha's for dinner. I shouldn't be that late."

"I've been on my own for a lot of years, Nico."

"I know, just lock up after the last crew leaves."

"I will."

It was close to Gwen's bedtime by the time the last of the men working on the house let her know they were leaving.

"Thank you," Emerald said watching as they got into their trucks. Locking the door, she made a beeline to the kitchen. It had been off limits all day, but the men that just left assured her it was finished.

Propping the kitchen door open to reveal what had been done to her kitchen, Emerald was stunned. The room was not even close to the same room she and Gwen had had breakfast in that morning.

How it was even possible was another question. The appliances were all brand new. The counters were replaced, the cabinets looked custom made to fit the vast space. An island in the center of the room was a new addition. Even the floor was new.

"Impossible," she said, opening every cabinet and drawer. Shifters were stronger and faster and there had been a lot of people working all day in her home, but this was insane.

"Gwen, do you have Mommy's phone?" She called to the three-year-old, who was hopefully winding down for the day. She needed to call Nico to thank him.

"It dead," Gwen called.

"Where is it so I can plug it in?" she said, entering the Living room. The phone sitting next to the couch was indeed dead, so Emerald went to plug it in.

Glancing out of the kitchen window, Emerald thought she saw movement. It was still light out this time of year for at least another hour. Craning her neck to see who it was, she saw nothing. It wasn't uncommon to spot a shifter in Wolf form going for a run.

It could be one of the workers who forgot something or it could be that Nico sent someone to watch her while he was gone. The second option seemed like something he would do.

The sound of the most recent Princess movie coming to an end made Emerald glance at the clock. It was only seven, but it seemed later for some reason. She had another hour before Gwen went down, and who knows how long Nico would be?

The house seemed weirdly empty after all of that day's activities. With no dishes to put away, no floor to mop, and no toys strewn all over, Emerald left the gleaming new kitchen and was halfway to the Living room to sit with Gwen.

"Nice place you have here," a woman's voice came from the room she had just been in, startling Emerald just as Gwen turned to ask for another movie.

"Thank you," Emerald said after a long silence, knowing exactly who was behind her. She turned slowly, placing herself between the woman and her daughter.

There in the center of the kitchen, in full view of the hallway Emerald was now in, was Cora.

"Cora, what are you doing here? If you're looking for Nico, he left." Emerald wanted to sound calm and not alarm Gwen. The three-year-old did the one thing she hoped she wouldn't.

"Mommy, the bad lady in the kitchen," she said while rushing to Emerald, putting herself closer to the bad lady than Emerald wanted.

"Yes, I know," Emerald said, crouching close to the three-year-old, speaking as softly as possible into her ear. "I need you to stay quiet while Mommy talks to Cora. *Run Gwen, Stranger danger,*" she whispered while making it look like she was kissing the toddler's cheek.

Thank god her daughter was smart. The term "*Stranger danger*" had been drilled into her since she could walk. Stay quiet, run away, get help. Emerald had hopefully instilled that response because Gwen was in danger. Emerald didn't know if Cora was after Nico or her, or maybe she knew how much Gwen meant to Nico and would use that.

13

For tense moments, Cora just stood there. Emerald knew she didn't stand a chance if the woman wanted to harm her. Cora was insane if she was willing to break into a home like this. She had to be off her meds, if shifters even had meds. All Emerald could think about was Gwen.

Emerald's little girl was heading for the door, but Cora was looking in that direction. The open kitchen doorway saw straight into the hallway Emerald was standing in. The same hallway that led to the front door, a door she had locked. The only other door Gwen could use was in back. That would mean going through the kitchen. Praying her daughter could unlock the door, Emerald needed to distract the woman in her home.

"Cora, why are you here?" Emerald said in a loud voice, stepping closer to the doorway, hopefully blocking the way.

Waving her hand behind her back in a gesture she hoped to god that Gwen would understand, she kept talking.

"Are you seriously just going to stand there and not say anything? I assume you broke into my home for a reason."

"I came to talk."

"Talk to me or Nico? As I said, he went home."

"He was here last night, then all day today."

"If you know that, then you know he already left for home. You also know that he was here but I wasn't last night. I went out last night with Jett."

Emerald took another step toward the woman, blocking the doorway completely as she felt the draft from the front door being opened. Smart girl, she thought. Now, she had to buy her daughter time. Town was two miles away. That was a long way for a three-year-old to go on her own. Gwen might just run a few feet and hide, or she could look for help. Emerald had no idea what the three-year-old would do. She had no assurance help was coming.

"Why was he here all day then?"

"I was having renovations done. He was here to oversee the work. You can still smell the paint and smell the wood. If you noticed he was here, then you saw the twenty other men and woman coming and going. How did you get in?"

"Back door was unlocked."

Suggesting she use it to leave was Emerald's first thought, then she decided against it. Gwen was outside. That meant she needed to keep Cora inside.

"And you just waltzed in and made yourself at home."

"Nico is mine," she was growling now, not good.

"I think that would be something you would need to talk to him about."

"Do you think I'm stupid?" the woman asked. It was a loaded question. Shifters could tell when a person was lying. So far, Emerald had been very careful with her answers.

"I try not to think of you at all, Cora."

"You smell of him."

"Of Nico?" Emerald sniffed her underarms and shrugged.

"Quit playing with me. His scent is all over you."

"He was here all day, Cora. We sat next to each other. He hugged me goodbye when he left because we are friends."

"I'm his mate."

"If you are his mate, then why are you here in my house uninvited? Nico has a number of female friends. Are you planning to visit them as well? I told you he went home."

"I saw him leave." Emerald's heart raced. Nico had left nearly two hours before, after an early supper.

"That was hours ago. "

"I heard he called his other whores and told them he found his mate." Cora's eyes didn't look right as she stepped closer to Emerald.

"Problem solved then." Emerald didn't like the woman's proximity to her new shiny knife rack. Nico obviously had to have lessons on child proofing.

"No, my problem is just starting because I think he meant you."

"Me? I'm human." All true statements, but it was getting harder stretching the truth.

"You are human. You already had a mate. You have a child. You are not his mate, I am."

"You already said that."

"You made him doubt me. You made him tell the Alpha that I threatened him."

"You should probably not have threatened your mate. I didn't have anything to do with telling anyone. You did. Jett, the man I had dinner with, he was the one that overheard you threaten the Alpha second. I believe he said others were there as well. It wasn't me." Emerald took a quick glance at the clock. It had only been five minutes. That meant only maybe three since Gwen left.

"You had dinner with Jett and Cole. Now you are trying to take my mate. That makes you nothing but a whore."

"I'd have to sleep with them to qualify, to be an actual whore, then I would have to ask them for money. Yes, I think money is involved to qualify. Even then, the times have changed, Cora. I have not slept with any men in four years."

That was the truth.

"I got here in time then." Cora's face morphed into a creepy stalkers face: part wolf, part human, all insane.

"In time for what?"

"In time to assure you don't tempt my mate with your scent."

"I'm not sure what that means. I'm human, remember?"

Reminding Cora that she was human was intentional. The woman had clearly expressed a dislike for humans and treated Emerald as inferior. The more Emerald could make herself look harmless, the better.

"Your scent, I can still smell your desire for my mate."

"Gross," Emerald exclaimed.

"You're ripe for the taking and unworthy of carrying an Alpha male's child."

"Again, gross, I just told you I haven't had sex with any man, Alpha or otherwise, in years, Cora."

"He is my mate, not yours." Cora was getting agitated.

"I don't recall saying he was mine." Emerald chose her words carefully.

"Where is the little one?" Cora glanced past Emerald to look into the hallway.

"She's three and human. Surely, you are not threatened by her. My understanding of this Mating thing is unclear, mostly, but I do know that it has nothing to do with my child."

Emerald walked further into the kitchen. The front door was wide open and there hadn't been enough time for a three-year-old to get very far if she was still running. In theory, Gwen was taught to run and get help. What anyone would do in a dangerous situation was hard to say, until you were in that situation. Gwen usually wanted her mother when upset. Hopefully, she wouldn't turn back.

"I am not threatened by your child or you for that matter. I'm not threatened by anyone."

"Then, why are you in my kitchen?" Emerald was past her initial fear. Now, she was just pissed. This woman invaded her home and threatened her child.

"I'd tone it down if I were you."

"And I'd run if I were you. I am the Alpha's assistant, Pack protected, and you just broke into my house uninvited, looking for a man that isn't here. A man that has made it clear he doesn't want you. "

The last part was a mistake and Emerald knew it. At this point, Emerald would do anything to keep Cora there. Gwen was outside somewhere. It was getting darker by the second and Cora looked like she had had enough banter.

"And you think he wants you?" Cora stepped away from the new island and the shiny knives and leaned against the sink behind her.

"I never said that, did I? To your knowledge, has he ever even dated a human?" Emerald took another step, fearing the woman might bolt out the back door and go after Gwen.

"No, he never has, until maybe now. I'm starting to get the idea that you are a big part of the reason Nico is denying my claim."

"The claim that you're pregnant?"

"True matings often result in conception," Cora bragged.

"I did hear that recently."

"So, what you need to do is leave my mate alone."

"Your mate has nothing to do with me. He is not here."

"His scent is everywhere. I don't like it. He is attached to you."

"I assume we are still talking about Nico. I work at the Pack house. I'm attached to everyone there and a few others here in the pack as well. It's called making friends."

14

Emerald expected Cora to argue, but she didn't. Instead, she said nothing. That was not a good sign. Her eyes had gone golden and her face contorted with rage. She was a predator and had played with her prey long enough. Emerald was well aware that she was the prey.

Emerald didn't stand a chance against this woman. Even if Cora had been human, she was larger and more toned. All Emerald could do at this point was stall and give Gwen as much time as possible to get away. This wasn't going to end well, but she wasn't going down without a fight. She was closer to the knives than Cora was, but Cora was still faster. The salt shaker on the island was to her left and the knives on the counter to her right.

Taking the salt shaker in her left hand, she looked up at Cora.

"What is it you think your going to do with that, Human?" Cora laughed as Emerald unscrewed the cap, hoping she didn't notice.

"Just checking to see if it needs to be refilled," Emerald quipped then tossed it at her while feigning to the right and grabbing the first knife in the rack. It wasn't the largest, but it wasn't the smallest either. It would have to do.

"Do you really expect to win with that?"

"I was hoping I wouldn't have to fight at all, Cora. I have a right to protect myself."

"You are a plague on my kind. Why the Alpha agreed to house the humans with that abomination, Blythe, is beyond me, but you working in his home, deciding who gets to see him and who needs to wait, is a joke. I know you set me up the other day."

"I set you up?" Emerald held the knife, realizing she had no clue how to defend herself against a Wolf shifter, even in Human form. She wasn't sure she could even use the knife if needed.

"You knew Nico was in with the Alpha and didn't warn me."

"It isn't my job to warn you. I told you he was in a meeting and you insisted. You're just looking to blame this on me because I'm human."

"You are to blame. Nico's interest in you is a problem. He told the others he found his mate. The thought of him meaning anyone other than me is sickening. The thought that he might be referring to you is unacceptable."

"Again, this is something you should talk to him about. I have not mated with anyone. Your super-shifter nose should be able to tell that."

"That only means there's still time to claim my mate."

Emerald didn't see it coming until it was too late. The back hand of an angry shifter hurts like hell. Sheer will, kept her standing upright. Her cheek was on fire, her jaw maybe broken. The cell phone she had plugged in caught her eye. In retrospect, she should have gone for that first. The phone was ancient and charged slowly, but she might have managed to hit 911. She wasn't even sure the number of emergencies in the area worked this deep into the forest.

Swiping blindly, she screamed anything she could think of. Cora landing the first blow told her that she wasn't going to win this, not even close. Her only goal was to give it all she had. The longer she stayed upright, the more time Gwen had.

"I am Pack protected. You will be banished," Emerald slurred, having trouble even speaking at all.

"I am the Alpha second's mate." She lunged and easily took the knife from Emerald, breaking her wrist in the process.

"Stop, you don't want to do this," Emerald screamed, clutching her broken wrist with her other hand. "They will kill you."

"I have a right to defend my position. Shifters fight to the death over their mates."

"I am not a shifter," Emerald cried. The pain threatening to take her under as she felt a second blow to her head. This time, she was knocked across the room from the sheer power of a deranged, Shifter female.

Unable to stand, Emerald slid down the wall until she was sitting on her beautiful, new floor.

"You are what stands between me and my mate. It's a justified kill."

By Lynn Leite

The word kill sent a rush of terror through Emerald. The woman was not going to stop. Emerald was going to have to fight with everything she had.

With blinding speed, Cora jerked Emerald up, gripping her shoulders until Emerald could feel Cora's breath in her face. Emerald had lost her sight in one eye. Her jaw was not broken, but her cheek was. The cold, slick sensation of the knife she had once used to defend herself penetrated her abdomen twice at least. Struggling and trying to inflict pain on her attacker was just making things worse.

Going limp was not a voluntary decision. At least, it wasn't her mind's decision. Her body had other ideas. Emerald was beyond pain. Her breathing was slowing mostly because one of the stab wounds pierced her lung.

A distant howl stopped Cora from doing further damage. She had already done plenty. Emerald could feel the life draining out of her. The fight in her was gone, not that she could actually fight. Curled on her new kitchen floor in an ever-increasing pool of her own blood, she saw fear on the face of her attacker.

Someone was coming and Gwen would be safe. It felt like she was watching someone else's life. Cora glanced down at her and Emerald kept as still as possible. The woman could hear her heartbeat, but even Emerald could tell it had slowed.

The moment Cora came to the realization that this was not going to end well was all over her face. Emerald didn't speak wolf. She didn't speak shifter, but whatever that howl had said to her attacker, made her shake. She was furiously washing the blade as if that was going to help. The water shut off and Emerald heard her footsteps as she rushed past her to search the Living room.

She was looking for Gwen. The rage Emerald felt in that moment was beyond anything she had ever felt. Nico would take care of her daughter. If he couldn't, then Blake and Alice would see to it.

The life she thought she would have that morning was looking dimmer by the second. She was human and broken. She lost count of how many times Cora had plunged the knife into her. It seemed an odd weapon for a shifter who could have shifted and eaten her or something. If Emerald hadn't grabbed the weapon in the first place, Cora might have eaten her. This was a better way to die, by far.

Emerald's mind was jumping from one thing to another as she heard the howl again. It was Nico. He was calling her. Either that, or a real wolf was just looking for his mate. She liked to think it was Nico. Hearing the sound of the back door slamming gave Emerald little hope. The phone was on the counter just above her feet. It might as well have been on the moon at that point.

If she moved too much, she'd bleed out faster. If she didn't move, she might not have much more time anyway. Her face hurt, her wrist throbbed, and she could feel herself draining of energy. Ironically, the knife wounds were the least painful of all her wounds.

Crawling across the floor in what looked to be all of her blood, she tried to pull up on one of the chairs only to collapse, facing the opposite direction.

"God, please watch over Gwen and Nico?" she said just as the pain from trying to move hit in a wave that ended in blackness.

15

"Mr. Nico… help, Mr. Nico?" The faint sound of Gwen crying hit his ears as Nico waited back at the Pack house. Alice was just pulling up to the home and jumped out of her car, looking at him.

"Was that Gwen calling?" she asked.

"I don't know." Nico searched the street and started running toward where the sound of Gwen's voice had come from.

"I'll get my bag," Alice called after him.

"Gwen, where are you?" he called, stopping to hear the answer.

"Mr. Nico?" The cry was faint but closer than it had been.

"I'm coming, Gwen, keep yelling." He smelled the air to help locate his soon to be daughter.

"I here. I here," she screamed. Her little voice was hoarse.

The exhausted three-year-old in her night clothing came running when Nico spotted her.

"Baby, what are you doing out here?"

"The bad... the bad... Stranger danger... I runned."

"The bad what, Gwen?"

"The bad lady was there. Mommy told me 'Stranger danger'. I runned."

"Alice, it's Cora. She is at Emerald's house."

"I'm right behind you," Alice yelled back.

Scooping up the three-year-old, he told her to hang on. He hadn't needed to. Gwen was clinging to him as if her life depended on it.

Running toward possible danger with the child was not an ideal choice, but he needed Alice, just in case Emerald needed Medical attention.

"Nico, stop," Alice came running after him. She had smelled the blood, so had Nico.

"Gwen needs to stay out here. I will go in," Alice pointed to the wide-open front door.

"She can't be gone," Nico said, putting Gwen down in the front hall. "I need you to stay right here, Baby."

"The bad lady inside?"

"I need to go see. Gwen, stay here. Don't open this door. Do you understand?"

"I under hand."

"Close enough," Nico said following Alice into his worst nightmare.

"Call Eli, tell him to send everyone." Alice looked up from Emerald, who was so still and covered with blood.

"Is she…"

"She's breathing. Call quickly, I'm going to need your help."

Nico was numb, going through the motions of putting out an alert. Alice was working on Emerald, who hadn't so much as groaned.

"Mommy?" Gwen's voice pierced his heart. He didn't have the strength to scold her for not following his directions.

"She's got a boo boo. Ms. Alice needs to fix her." Nico was crying. Alpha shifters rarely cried. His life was on the floor of the newly renovated kitchen. He was torn between staying by her side or hunting down the woman that did this."

"Gwen, do you know where Mommy keeps her shirts?"

"I do," Gwen answered Alice.

"Can you go pick out the biggest, prettiest ones for me?"

"I can." Gwen, having something to do, ran up the stairs.

Nico looked panicked.

"We would sense if Cora was still here, Nico. I need you to choose."

"Choose what? What are you talking about?"

"She's dying, Nico. I can't do much here and she won't survive the trip to the Clinic. If you turn her, she stands a chance."

"Then, I will."

"Nico, she still might not live. If you bite her, you will be officially mated. If she dies and we lose you too..."

"I need your word you will take care of Gwen." Nico knew that Gwen's care, if they both died, was his only obstacle. He was already prepared to follow Emerald if she passed.

"I will raise her as my own, but I won't have to. You will both live. The Universe can't be that cruel."

"One more thing."

"Anything."

"Cora dies."

"She's already marked for death. I declare it."

"Thank you, where is safe to bite so I don't hurt her further?"

"Nico, she doesn't feel anything right now, I promise you. Do it now. I'm going to check on Gwen and give you some privacy."

This was not the way he had planned to claim his mate. He still hadn't gotten an answer as to whether she wanted to turn. She had accepted his claim, he thought. He was secure in that fact. His turning her might make her mad, but she'd be alive. The scent of blood was overwhelming as he bent, biting her on the shoulder, pausing with his mouth on her, on the off-chance it would help the transition go faster.

The front door of Emerald's house crashing in would have had him on alert if he hadn't called in the troops. Ghost, along with his brother Chance, made one hell of an entrance.

"Holy shit!" Ghost stopped short of the doorway.

"Check the perimeter, then find that bitch. She's mine, Ghost."

"I hear you. Sir, I can call Jazz to help. She can be here in moments. Where is the little girl?"

"She's upstairs with Alice. Call Blythe. She will make arrangements for tonight. Jazz doesn't strike me as maternal."

"She'd better be. We are expecting."

"Congrats."

"Sir, do you think we should move her?" Ghost cautiously asked. Nico could only imagine what the scene looked like.

"Not until I'm sure it's safe. Go find Cora."

Nico was aware when more men entered the house. He knew that Eli and the guard was right behind Ghost and Chance.

"Oh god, shit, Jenkins, find the Alpha. Call Lincoln. He was having dinner with the Shadow Pack Alpha," Eli said, pointing to the door. "Nico, what do you need?"

Eli was a good man. He handled crises well. That was a good thing, because Nico was holding on by a thread.

"I need Alice. She's upstairs. I need you to help keep Gwen safe. I am not sure what to do with Gwen right now."

"I've got that handled. I'll get Alice and make sure Gwen is safe. I need to know what happened here. Do you know who did this?"

"Cora, she did this."

"Because Emerald is human?"

"Because she's mine. It could be because she's human as well. Better put a guard on the other humans."

"I will handle it. Stay with your mate. She needs you now."

"Thank you, Eli."

16

"Nico, Gwen needs you to tell her it's safe to go with Ellery," Alice said as she checked the wounds on Emerald's stomach for the tenth time.

"I'm covered with blood," Nico said as if he had just noticed.

"Here." Blake stripped his own shirt off and handed it to Nico. Nico hadn't even realized that his Alpha had arrived.

Taking a deep breath and schooling his features, he went out into the front hall where Ellery was speaking softly to Gwen.

"Hey Gwen, Miss Alice said you were scared to go with Ellery. You know Ellery, right?"

"I stay with you. You be my Daddy."

"I need to take care of Mommy with Miss Alice so she can get all better."

"You love Mommy?" Gwen was verging on tears. She had been holding it together far better than Nico thought possible.

"Yes, Gwen, I love Mommy and I love you. I won't let anything else happen to you ever again. Right now, I need you to go with Miss Ellery. You did good. You got help. You are a brave girl.

"We are going to go have a sleepover at Blythe's. How does that sound?" Ellery tried to sound cheerful.

"I want Mommy."

"I know, Baby. I need you to go with Ellery, just for tonight." Nico didn't know if he could handle it if Gwen started sobbing harder.

"Mommy be better a-marrow?"

"I don't know for sure," Nico refused to lie to Gwen.

"Come on, Gwen, I see you have a pretty pink bag here. Do you need a pillow?" Ellery asked to get her moving.

"I have my stuffy."

"Alright, then we are off. Susanne's driving me. Nico, you don't have to worry."

"Thank you." Nico kissed Gwen's head and watched as Ellery walked her to the car that Susanne was in.

"Is it safe to move her yet? I can't stand seeing her on this floor."

"I think we can move her. I just didn't want Gwen here to see it. Jett is backing up a truck so we can get her to the Clinic. I need to see what's going on inside. Her wounds are extensive and she was human when she sustained them."

"Is she turning? Is it working?"

"I can't be sure, but I think so."

"You think so?" Nico screeched.

"Nico," Blake scolded.

"Sorry, Alpha, Alice."

"It's forgiven and I do see signs of healing. I'm considering a second bite," Alice continued.

"From me?" Nico didn't know if he could handle Blake biting his mate.

"Yes, I'm not risking you tearing Blake's head off and making me a widow. Your bite seems to be working, just not as fast as I'd like. I would like to X-ray her to see what's going on inside before we speed up any healing. The bones in her face and her wrist are broken. I don't know what else."

"I'll do anything."

"We know," Blake said, placing a hand on his friend's shoulder.

Moving Emerald was excruciating. Alice swore she couldn't feel it, but Nico did. Often, Mated shifters can sense the other's pain or strong emotions. Nico wasn't sure if what he was feeling was actually her pain or his reaction to seeing her injuries?

"The X-ray will show the damage. Theo and Faith are on their way. We are going to save her, Nico." Susanne had met them at the Clinic after making sure Gwen was safely with the others. Susanne had been training with Alice at the Clinic when she wasn't on Guard duty. She was trying to assure him.

"She has to live," he said, waiting as Alice took the X-ray. He had trouble leaving her on the table like that, but Alice assured him that the X-ray wouldn't take long."

"Nico, can I get you anything, something to drink?" Blake was at a loss as to what to do himself.

"I'm fine." Nico knew it was a lie. He wasn't fine.

The wolf inside was trying to tear free and hunt. Cora was dead, either by his hand or by one of the guards. Nico didn't care, but his wolf did. The human, the man, needed to stay with Emerald. He needed to hear her breathing, breathe her scent. He had bitten her, claimed her. She was his.

Theo, the Doctor from the Shadow Pack rushed in along with his co-worker, Faith. Alice had trained under the man, who had more experience and more knowledge about Shifter medicine, as well as Human medicine, than anyone else in the Tri-pack area.

"Nico?" Blake snapped at him.

"What?"

"You were growling and your eyes were going. Theo is a Mated male and your mate's best hope."

"I didn't realize."

"I know. Your wolf is on the surface. I command you to let Theo work on your mate." An Alpha order couldn't be denied by the man or the wolf.

"Thank you, I was losing it."

"I could see that. I get it. She's hurt."

"She's bleeding out and beaten, Blake."

"She's alive right now. You need to hang on to that."

"I am trying. I'm worried about Emerald. I feel like I should be with her. I need to be in there."

"And you will be, as soon as Theo and Alice say it's safe."

"Has anyone heard from Ellery? How is Gwen?"

"I will call and check. Eli left June on guard inside and Eli has Parker, Cole, and Jenkins surrounding the house."

"Who is looking for Cora?"

"Ray, Otto, Jett, and Elliot are out there with Ghost and his brother. I have guards from both the Moon Valley and the Shadow Pack on alert. The wards haven't been disturbed. I checked with the Coven to make sure," Blake answered."

"Thank you."

"We have got everything else covered. All you need to do is concentrate on Emerald."

"She's going to be pissed."

"That you saved her?"

"No, I don't think she will be upset that she's turned. She was considering it. She will be pissed that Cora got the better of her."

"It was Human vs Shifter and a crazy shifter at that. Emerald didn't stand a chance."

"Why didn't I see this coming?"

"No one thought Cora would go this far," Blake felt a bit of guilt himself.

"I think that Emerald will be grateful that we turned her. The alternative is not good. Think of it this way, now, if anyone else attacks her, she can kick ass," Susanne offered.

"Maybe, we should save Cora's execution for her?" Nico growled.

"She wouldn't be able to do it. She couldn't hurt a fly. I'm not sure how she will feel about Cora's Death sentence, even if she thinks she deserves it." Blake was right. Emerald might not understand. Not that that was going to save Cora. She attacked a Pack protected human in her home.

By Lynn Leite

17

"The bones are set, the internal damage stitched, and she is healing. A second bite wouldn't hurt."

A man was talking, but Emerald couldn't place the voice. She was awake, sort of, surprised to even be alive. There was a strange ringing in her ears and a whole lot of voices she didn't recognize, not just the man. Thinking about what happened, she expected it to be fuzzy, bits and pieces of the attack. Instead, she got full color images and a blow-by-blow reenactment in her head as she slipped back under into a dreamless sleep.

She was aware that some time had passed since the last time she had awakened. The sounds were different and she sensed less people were in the room.

"Gwen," she croaked, thinking that her little girl was out there and the monster lunatic, Cora, had gone out not long after.

"I think she's waking up," Alice said. The comfort of hearing a familiar voice did wonders to her spirit.

"Hey, are you going to sleep all day?" Nico, she knew that silky tone as well.

"Gwen," she tried again and it came out in a whisper.

"She's with Ellery and the ladies at the Bed and Breakfast. She's safe. She saved your life," Alice told her.

"I died?"

"Almost, maybe a little," Nico said as Emerald felt the bed she was in dip and Nico's body press against her carefully. Just feeling him there next to her calmed her chaotic mind.

"Cora?"

"We know. Gwen was very clear that it was the bad lady. We have people out looking for her. Can you open your eyes? I need to see them, Emerald?"

Emerald opened them slowly, surprised that they worked. She had one practically swollen shut when she passed out.

"How long?"

"A day and a half," Alice answered," can you tell me how you feel?"

"Like I died. I was bleeding out... my head was..." Emerald lifted a hand and touched her head, feeling no pain.

"I can't say for sure whether you were dead at one point, but you are not now."

"Emerald, I have to tell you something. I had to bite you. There was no other way to save you."

"You bit me."

"Twice, actually."

"I thought I heard a man say that."

"That was Theo, the Doctor from the Shadow Pack. He just left."

"I'm a shifter?"

"Yes, your Shifter side has been working hard to repair what happened. We had to reset bones in your face. The wounds to your abdominal were extensive. We stitched you up internally to help you heal. You should make a full recovery with no complications."

"I was worried. I was hearing things. The voice in my head isn't me going insane, good to know," Emerald said, sounding exhausted.

"You need rest. Shifter healing is good, but it still takes time. You were on the brink of death, so rest is what the Doctor orders."

"Can I go home? I need to see Gwen."

"You can go home this afternoon, but you need to stay in bed."

"I will bring Gwen here if you want, or we can ask Sussanne to bring her to the house," Nico offered.

"The house, I don't know if I'm up to watching her. So, maybe just a visit."

"You have a mate who can watch our daughter until your well enough to tell me I'm doing it all wrong," Nico's words made Emerald cry.

"You bit me, but…"

"The rest is just a formality. Blake already sanctioned our mating. It's official."

"And I slept through it."

"You were fighting for your life at the time."

Just sitting up made Emerald feel like she had run a marathon. Glancing down at her stomach, the thin pink lines where the knife had gone in were almost healed. Healing from the memory of the event was going to take time.

"Emerald, can you tell me what happened?" Blake's soft voice resonated within her. She knew enough about shifters to know that was her wolf responding to its Alpha.

"I was curious about what had been done in my kitchen. Nico hadn't let me go in there all day. I expected a new dishwasher not an entire kitchen."

"Where was Gwen?" Nico asked.

"She was watching her third Princess movie. I was on my way out of the kitchen because I heard her movie ending when Cora said something from behind me. I locked the front door but apparently not the back door."

"None of this is your fault."

"I know that. I knew there was no way she was there for a chat. All I could think was I hope Gwen doesn't see her."

"But she did?"

"Yes, I whispered to her, hoping she listened the thousand times I told her about dangerous people."

"Stranger danger," Nico nodded.

"Yes, I had to hope she got away. I had to distract Cora. I was the one that grabbed the knife."

"You were defending yourself," Alice comforted.

"By the way, Nico, leaving a set of sharp knives on a counter with a three-year-old in the house isn't a great idea."

"Duly noted," he nodded.

"Cora is a shifter. I knew I wouldn't win in a fight. I was just trying to buy time."

"What did she say about why she was there?"

"She said Nico was her mate. I guess she figured out that I was the person he meant when he told the others he had found a mate. I tried telling her that I had not had sex even once in the last, almost four years. I hoped her Shifter Spicy senses would tell I was being truthful."

"Shifter Spicy senses?" Nico smiled.

"I don't know. It seemed like a good comparison. She didn't buy it. She hit me, then, when I didn't go down, she took the knife I had," Emerald lifted her right-hand, twisting the wrist that seemed to be working just fine.

"I set the bones. Take it easy on that wrist for a couple of days," Alice stopped her from rolling the wrist anymore.

"Right, so, after that, she hit me hard and I don't remember much after that. I knew I was being stabbed. It occurred to me that she could have shifted and just eaten me. Using the knife was a more Human thing to do."

"She won't be using anything anymore," Nico growled.

"Did you find her?"

"Not yet, it's just a matter of time."

"Then what, is their Shifter jail?"

"There is a sort of Shifter jail but not for Cora. She's has been marked for death."

"Okay. I think I need to lie down now." Emerald had been sitting for maybe three or four minutes and she was exhausted.

"I'm going to take you home. You can rest in your own bed," Nico lifted her into his arms and carried her to a waiting vehicle.

"You're sure Gwen is alright?"

"You let me worry about Gwen for now. She's safe and has a guard. I won't ever let anything happen to either of you again."

"You can't make that promise, Nico."

"I just did."

18

Emerald had fallen asleep on the short ride to her home. It wasn't until Nico started to carry her into the front door that she panicked.

"Emerald?" Nico said, holding her tightly as she started to wriggle out of his arms.

"I… what if she's back?" Emerald said, feeling her chest tighten.

Nico sat on the top step and held her against him. He knew that if he let go, she was going to bolt or, even worse, shift for the first time. Alice had been clear that she should wait a day or two before exerting herself. Emerald had assumed that the woman had meant sexual activity, but Alice had assured them that would be alright in a few hours, as long as they took it easy. What Alice had meant was shifting.

"Emerald, she's not here. She is no match for me. You are a shifter now, just listen."

"Listen?"

"Yes, listen, tell me what you hear?"

Emerald stopped and listened. She heard her heartbeat and Nico's. It was strange hearing her own and his was louder than she expected."

"Heartbeats," she said softly.

"How many?" Nico asked.

Emerald strained, listening to hers then Nico's, straining to hear one no two more farther away.

"Four, ours and two more," she scanned the woods looking like a terrified animal.

"The one in that direction is Parker," he said as Emerald took deep, calming breaths, trying to ward off the panic attack she was heading toward. "The other is Susanne. You'll get used to identifying people as time goes on. They were here in the house. I can tell by their scents. I had them scout ahead and clean up a bit."

"The kitchen... I bled a lot. It has to be a mess," Emerald wasn't sure she could face that.

"Yes, it was a mess and it's all taken care of. The kitchen is safe. You are safe. You're here and we are going to make sure Cora never hurts anyone again."

"Is Blake really going to have her killed? Is that even legal?"

"It's Shifter law. She lost her right to exist. She attacked you and threatened my mate in the process."

"I think she really believes you are hers."

"She has nothing to base that claim on. Even if she believes that to be true, she had no right attacking you. If she believed I was hers, there were others she knew I was seeing. She knew that and didn't feel threatened by them. She targeted you, no one else. I was a fool to believe dating multiple women was the right way to find a mate."

"I do believe I might have told you that a time or two."

"If you had just shook my hand all those months ago, I would have known you were mine the moment you started working for Blake."

"And I would have told you to go suck an egg. I am human."

"You were human."

"Fine, I was human and you were so cocky. I needed to see the real you: the Nico that was so good with Gwen, the Nico that said hello to me every morning and brought me lunch twice a week. I needed to see that man or I would have told you to go to hell."

"Have I earned your trust? I know you said yes to my claim, but you had no say when I bit you."

"You have earned my trust and my love. I love you, Nico."

"That's good to hear because you are stuck with me. Your eyes are drooping again. Can we go inside now? I'll tuck you in so you can rest. "

"Will you check on Gwen?"

"I'll do one better. I'll have June and Jenkins escort Ellery and bring her here."

"I need to see her."

"I know and she needs to see you."

Emerald looked away as they passed the door to her new kitchen. It was going to be a while before she felt safe in her own house. She needed new locks, maybe an alarm system and cameras, yes, cameras.

"You look worried," Nico said, picking up on her thoughts.

"I know that I'm safe, that you will keep me safe, but..."

"But you want more security. I already hired a team to install cameras and change the locks. Let me know if you want me to call the Coven and have them ward the house."

"Ward the house?"

"Yes, it's an invisible barrier that would surround the property. There are ways to make it so that we would know when someone passed through."

"Security cameras and new locks should be enough."

"You can let me know if you change your mind. It's going to be a while before you're comfortable. I had an idea."

"What idea?"

"Eli has a group that comes and trains in hand-to-hand combat. They meet at the Senior center a couple of times a week. Until you are used to your wolf and used to shifting, you could train with them. Cora was only able to harm you because you were human. She wouldn't stand a chance with a Shifter female."

"Way to make a girl feel inferior." Emerald was half joking as Nico lay her down on her bed.

"You are far from inferior. You are brave and strong. You survived an attack where you were outmatched in strength and speed. You are not outmatched any longer. Cora is marked for death. She was in the wrong. If she ever gets close to you again, which she won't, but if she did, you could easily kill her, Emerald."

"I can't even stay awake for very long right now. I can't kill a fly."

"You are healing, coming back from the brink of death. Sleeping it off so you can heal for a day or two is all you need."

"Will you lay with me until I fall asleep?"

"I've been waiting a long time for you to invite me into your bed," Nico grinned.

"Sleeping is all I can promise you right now."

"I would wait a lifetime, Emerald, as long as you're okay. That's all that matters right now. I'm sorry this had to happen."

"Not the way you planned to spend the night of your mating?"

"Not even close."

"I promise tomorrow night will be different."

"Get some rest. I plan on proving to you that you and I were meant to be."

"I already know that, Nico," Emerald said softly as sleep pulled at her once again.

"I'm going to make you mine in every way possible."

"I'm looking forward to it," Emerald mumbled into the pillow.

By Lynn Leite

19

Coming awake with a startle, it took a second for Emerald to realize she was at home in bed. The sun was shining in the window like it did most mornings. It was morning, she thought as she felt the bed next to her for Nico. It was empty and cold. A brief moment wondering if it had all been a dream was interrupted by the sound of several people in her home. She closed her eyes, trying to listen like Nico had suggested.

One heartbeat directly below her that was in the kitchen, two in the Living room, one outside. The sound of yet another Princess movie flowed up the stairs so clearly, it was like Emerald was in the room.

The scent of food was making her mouth water. She couldn't recall the last time she ate. Scanning her belly, she saw the thin, pink lines were now nearly undetectable. A faint, white scaring was nearly gone as well.

Her wolf was hungry. A low growl startled her until she realized it was her own.

"Somebody is hungry," she smiled.

She hadn't been sure about turning when Nico first broached the subject. She knew a lot about shifters. She had learned even more since working for the Alpha. It was very different being one.

"Are you up here talking to yourself?" Nico leaned against the doorjamb in just a pair of drawstring pants.

"I was talking to my wolf. She's hungry."

"I'll bet. Alice is in the kitchen making something."

"Who is with Gwen?" Emerald asked, realizing that the two heartbeats were still in the Living room and one in the kitchen."

"Blake is with Gwen in the Living room. I went for a run. My wolf needed to get out."

"The Alpha is watching a Princess movie with my daughter?"

"She's *our* daughter now. She called me Daddy this morning instead of Mr. Nico and yes, he is watching a Princess movie and she painted his nails. He said it was good practice."

"Alice is pregnant?"

"Alice and Jazz, from what I hear. It's going to be a virtual baby boom."

"Four matings in just a few months will do that."

"I'm going to do my best to add you to the list of pregnant mates."

"Oh, and who said I was ready to have more children?"

"Gwen made sure I knew she wanted a little sister, not a little brother, because boys were yucky."

"And if we have a boy?"

"She will adjust. How are you feeling?"

"Amazing, actually, if I wasn't starving, I'd suggest we get right to work giving Gwen a sibling."

"Alice and Blake already offered to take Gwen to the park today," Nico winked.

"Did they catch Cora?"

"No, but trust me, the Alpha is the best bodyguard that Gwen could ever have."

"I trust Blake and Alice. I do need to see my daughter. I'm surprised she didn't jump on the bed when she got here."

"She did and you said 'Five more minutes, Gwen'. That was last night. I put her to bed and she woke up when Alice and Blake arrived."

"I need to see her and eat, then maybe tell her I need some private time with Mr. Nico."

"Daddy."

"I always said you'd make a great father."

"Then, all I have to do is convince you that I'm a great mate as well."

"I am nearly convinced." Emerald stood, taking inventory of all of the things that were broken and bleeding the night before last. "Shifter healing is incredible. I'm stiff, but I feel like nothing happened."

"You have Alice and the Shadow Pack Doctor to thank for that. I nearly tore the door down when Theo was doing surgery on you."

"Nico, Alice said I was a mess inside. Can I even have kids now?" Cora had targeted her abdomen over and over with the knife. Emerald wondered if that had been intentional.

"Yes, she said everything is in working order."

"You asked about kids?"

"I did."

"Are you trying to keep me barefoot and pregnant, Nico?" Emerald smiled as she took his hand on the stairs.

"Not at all, you can we wear shoes," he grinned.

"Mommy, you wake."

"Gwen, my brave girl, you did so good."

"Daddy say I save Mommy." Hearing Gwen call Nico Daddy nearly broke her resolve to be strong in front of her daughter. Her baby had a Daddy now, one that would never leave, one that would protect her with his life.

"He's right. You did save me."

"Come see, Mr. Blake has sparkles."

"Sparkles?" Emerald asked as Blake stood, coming out to the hallway. He did indeed sparkle. "Gwen, what did we say about glitter?"

"No litter until an abdult, Mr. Blake an abdult."

"She has a point," Nico smiled at the Alpha. "It suits you, Sir."

"I will be sure to clean it up," Blake assured Emerald.

"You apparently have zero experience with glitter, Blake. You don't clean up glitter. You learn to live with it." Emerald reached out, brushing the sparkles off of the Alpha's shoulder. "Maybe, shifting will help?"

"Speaking of shifting, you should try at some point, when you are feeling up to it."

"I will. Is it normal to be this exhausted from just walking down the stairs?"

"Nothing about what happened to you is normal. You are still physically healing and dealing with the attack. You paled just looking at the kitchen door."

"That was where Cora was."

"She's not there now. I can assure you," Nico said softly." Listen closely, use your new senses. How many heartbeats do you hear?"

"Five," she listened, honing in on each person's heartbeat.

"That's right. Alice and Blake, plus the three of us makes five. No one else is here."

"Is the back door locked?"

"Yes."

"Alright, then let's go look at my new kitchen."

Nico was impressed with his mate's strength. She faced her fears head on. Even in her weakened condition, she was the strongest person he knew.

20

"We have Gwen for the rest of the day. Ellery will keep her at Blythe's again tonight. By tomorrow, you should be much better," Alice told Emerald as she and Blake started to leave.

"I'm just tired. She can stay here. I don't want to bother anyone."

"Gwen is no bother. You and Nico need some time together and you need to shift. We will bring her back in the morning. Enjoy your mate and make sure you get some rest."

"I plan on it. Thank you, Alice."

"I need the practice," Alice glanced at Blake, who still had some sparkles in his hair.

"Gwen, be a good girl and listen to Ms. Alice and Ms. Ellery."

"I be good girl. We wost mores."

Nico looked to Emerald for an interpretation.

"They roasted smores," she explained.

"Be careful near the fire," Nico warned. He was taking to the role of a parent like she had imagined he would.

The house was empty, only two heartbeats anywhere near the place. Emerald thought she heard some faint sounds coming from far away. Her new hearing was going to take some getting used to.

"You look deep in thought." Nico came closer, turning her head gently until she was looking at him.

"I was thinking that I have a lot of adjusting to do."

"Do you mean adjusting to being a shifter or adjusting to being a Mated woman?"

"Both. plus, Gwen having a Daddy, she really latched on to that term quickly."

"She deserves a mother and a father. Do you know what else she deserves?"

"Brothers and sisters?" Emerald saw the gleam in Nico's eyes. She had seen the man look at plenty of women. Not one of them received the look that she was getting from him now.

"Exactly."

"Well, then we should get right on that," Emerald smiled.

"Are you up to it?"

"I'm more than up to it. I will warn you it's been a while. Gwen's Bio-Dad was the last person I was with."

"You are kidding me?" Nico exclaimed.

"No, I'm not."

"That means that every man you have met since then was an idiot. I think maybe you have a lot of catching up to do," Nico grinned.

"I'm not sure what you mean by that. I know your reputation, Nico, and I believe you when you said it was exaggerated. I'm pretty sure catching up would be impossible. The past, our pasts, they don't matter."

"That's right. When a shifter finds their true mate, it's game over. You are the only woman I will ever want for the rest of my life." Nico bent, taking her mouth in a gentle kiss.

"I have one request."

"Anything."

"Can we do this upstairs in a bed?"

"You thought I'd toss you on the floor right here in the hallway?"

"The thought occurred to me and, as sexy and adventurous as it sounds in theory, I am not ready for that kind of adventure just yet. I don't think the floor would be all that comfortable."

"Naked in bed it is, then maybe in the shower, on the couch…"

"All talk and no action," Emerald teased. Her body was already humming at the prospect of Nico making love to her. She had no doubt in her head that Nico was skilled in the arts of sexual seduction. She also had little doubt in her mind that he had never truly made love to any of the other women.

"Emerald, you are playing with fire. I want to be sure you are ready."

"I'm ready, willing and, according to Alice, able. Nothing hurts. I'm slightly tired right now, that's all. I should be dead, Nico. The fact that I'm not is something to celebrate."

"Take my hand," he said, offering his hand just as he had the first day they met. This time, she gladly took it. The hum of awareness warmed her body. She knew this man. She loved this man. Her wolf called to him.

Nico led her slowly up the stairs and to the bedroom she would now share. "You are so beautiful," he sighed, stopping once they were there to just look at her.

Emerald smiled, knowing he meant it. Her wolf sensed the truth. His heart remained steady and his breathing even. She had heard that shifters could sense a lie, now she felt it.

"Nico, I need you."

That was also the truth.

His kiss was a revelation. Her transformation meant she had senses beyond the Human ones she had always relied on. His scent filled her nose. His skin felt right against hers. The heat he put off was warming her down to her soul. She had already known that he was hers. Now, she felt it.

"Your eyes are glowing," Emerald said as Nico slowly stripped both of them.

"So are yours," he grinned pushing her gently down onto the bed.

The awkwardness she had expected never came. Nico took his time with her, exploring every hill and valley. She did the same. Mary Grace, one of the women that lived at the B&B, had nicknamed Nico "Tall, dark, and dangerous". He was dangerous, tall, and dark, but he was also kind, gentle, and delicious.

"Nico," Emerald exclaimed, surprised when he turned up the heat.

"I've got you. Let go, Emerald," he groaned.

"I don't want to let go. I want to hold on."

"Either way, you are mine now."

Nico picked up the pace. The feel of his mate was more than he had ever experienced and that was saying a lot. The connection between them seemed to snap into place as he took her up and over the precipice.

"Nico," she yelled, surprising herself. She had never screamed a man's name, ever.

"I love the sound of you screaming my name."

"I'd make some sort of smart comeback, but I can't even think right now."

"We are already in bed. Get some rest, I'm not going anywhere."

"Alice said I should shift."

"That takes a lot of energy. You can do it in the morning. I want you to be healed completely."

"I don't know if I will ever be completely over what happened."

"Your mind will realize you are not the same now. If that attack happened today, even with you being exhausted, you would win. You have the advantage."

"What advantage would I have? I've been a shifter for a couple of days. Cora was born that way."

"You have a mate to fight for and a child. Only the stupid gets between a Female shifter and her pup. Even Alpha males can be taken down by a protective female."

"I think that might apply in the Human world as well. You hear about women lifting cars to get to their child. You're saying that Cora's only advantage was that I was human?"

"Yes, that is exactly what I'm saying. They will find her and this will fade to the back of our lives. You might never forget completely. I'm not expecting you to."

"I will always remember that my mate had to bite me when I was unconscious."

"I can bite you again, if you like, but the last two bites are still healing."

"I will take a rain check on the biting."

"Anything you want, Emerald."

"Those are dangerous words, Nico. I want a lot."

"You deserve the world. Go to sleep. In the morning, we will get our daughter."

"I love the fact that you love her."

"I will love all of our children."

"That's right. I forgot about newly mated Shifter fertility," Emerald looked down at her flat belly. It was even flatter than it had been before she turned.

"We can take precautions from now on, if you're not ready."

"I'm more than ready, Nico."

"Good, because so am I."

21

"What do I do now? I feel exposed out here in nothing but a backpack." Emerald and Nico were both standing naked in her backyard so Emerald could learn to shift.

The backpack was a pack designed by some werewolf, tired of being naked after a shift. A shifter stripped down, putting the clothing in the pack, then putting it on their Human body. When they transformed, the pack remained on the wolf's back, thanks to some expandable straps.

Emerald's clothing was in her pack along with a pair of shoes. They were just running for a short while, but Nico thought it would be better for Emerald to get used to the pack as well as the shifting.

"Search for your wolf. She's there inside, waiting to come out."

"Should I get on all fours?"

"Emerald, have you ever seen one of us shift?"

"The Alphas mate, when I first got here, came to the door stripped down and shifted. It was pretty much a blur."

"And that's the last time you saw someone shift?"

"First and last, it's hard to argue that Wolf shifters don't exist when the proof is on the lawn. Gwen was one at the time. I almost dropped her."

"How did Gwen react?"

"She yelled "*Again*" while clapping her hands, "Emerald smiled.

"Then, she's going to love that Mommy can do the same thing. Let your wolf come forward. She's a part of you. You can feel her. She wants to run."

"I can feel her."

"Let her come to the surface."

"Will I still know what I'm doing?"

"She's part of you, not separate. You will know what is happening. I'll be right beside you."

"Alright, here goes." Emerald felt her wolf. The beast was strangely familiar. It was like her subconscious was just coming to life.

The stretching of her muscles as she changed was not uncomfortable at all. In fact, it felt good. She was falling forward as her arms stretched out, changing to paws. She blinked a few times, adjusting to the new perspective, then she took a step forward, falling on her face or snout, whatever it was.

"It takes some getting used to, I hear from other humans that were turned. Four legs instead of one," Nico said, still in his Human form. Emerald sat up, watching Nico as he flowed from the man to the wolf, with a grace she was sure she hadn't shown.

The hearing she had thought was accentuated before was even more honed in Wolf form. She could smell the forest, sense movement in the leaves. A squirrel darted out and she chased it without thinking about how to run on four legs. The wolf knew how and, as soon as Emerald stopped overthinking it, she was racing through the forest behind her home, jumping over fallen logs and weaving through the underbrush.

She could feel the pack on her back, but it seemed to weigh nothing. Nico stayed a step behind as she familiarized herself with her Canine side.

Nico gently guided her in a loop that led back to her home. As much as he wanted to run all day with her, they had Gwen coming home around Noon and needed to be home.

The transformation back to human was faster, words spilling out as soon as she was human again.

"Oh my god! What a rush. Did you smell the flowers? The air was sweet. I didn't know it could be like this. I was so aware of everything."

"I take it that you liked it," Nico smiled, taking his pack and retrieving the clothing he had in it. Emerald did the same.

"I felt so powerful, like part of the forest."

"You are powerful, Emerald."

"I dare Cora to show up now. I'll tear her to pieces." Emerald heard a low growl then realized it was coming from her.

"Slow down, Tiger."

"Is there any word? Did they ever find her?"

"No, and that's surprising. She's clearly hiding. Ghost will find her. He and his brother Chance are the best. She might have had a plan in place before she attacked you."

"You think it was premeditated?"

"I wouldn't doubt it. Her best chance of surviving is to lay low, disappear. The wards aren't disturbed, so she's still in the Tri-pack region."

"As long as she doesn't come near me."

"She'd be pretty stupid to do that."

"She was stupid to attack in the first place."

"True, I'm not sure what she thought killing me was going to do."

"She's not in her right mind, Emerald. If, like you said, she has convinced herself that I am her mate, then she's acting on pure instinct."

"She's convinced herself. She feels the pull, or does she really feel it?"

"If it had been real to her, she would have targeted all of the others, as well as you. You being human was why she chose you."

"Because she knew she would win."

"She didn't win and she won't in the end."

"I will feel better once they find her."

"We all will. In the meantime, I'm not going to keep from living life. Gwen is coming home this afternoon. I heard that the ladies at the B&B spoiled her a little."

"I'm sure they did."

22

A call from Blythe worried Emerald, looking at Nico as he spoke to the woman housing the Human women at her old Victorian that usually served as a Bed and Breakfast. This summer it was a place for the four humans that still had no idea they lived in a shifter pack to stay.

"What did she say?" Emerald asked. Nico looked concerned, not worried.

"Aya and Tasha are coming for a visit."

"Why?"

"Because you were injured enough to send your three-year-old to stay with Ellery at Blythe's."

"And I'm not injured anymore. How am I going to explain that I'm fine now? What were they told?"

"Blythe said that they were told that you started dating me. An old girlfriend was not happy with that. She broke in and you suffered a head injury that knocked you out. Gwen ran to get help."

"That is close to the truth. Gwen didn't mention the blood?"

"I don't know, but she's three. We can say she was exaggerating."

"Alright, head injury, having a concussion seems like an issue where I'd need watching and rest, and a three-year-old might need babysitting."

"That's our story and we are sticking with it, unless…"

"Unless what?" Emerald asked.

"Well, Blythe wanted me to know that Gwen told the women that her Daddy was a shipper."

"A shipper, not shifter."

"Right, I don't know what I ship, but I'm a shipper."

"Nico, she called you Daddy. I think they already knew you were dating more than one woman, now Gwen is calling you Daddy."

"Now, I'm with you. We can tell them I realized you were the love of my life. I wish the women would figure this out already. If they knew about shifters and the Mating pull, it would be easily explained that I'm her with you and Gwen's new Daddy."

"I wish they all knew, but I don't know the best way to do that. I was pretty freaked when the Alpha's mate just stripped down and poofed into a wolf. I didn't believe it at first, but I had been warned."

"The ladies have books that Alice brought to them. They think that the books are based on legends or pure fiction about shifters, Wolf shifters in particular. I've heard them talking when I visited the B&B. Ellery keeps trying to convince them that it could be true. She has always believed in the supernatural or paranormal. I'm not sure what shifters would be classified as," Emerald grinned.

"They need to make the connection soon. I can't have Eli's guards at the Victorian all the time. It is a favorite duty for the unmated males lately."

"Why?"

"Because of the Domino effect. An Alpha taking a mate usually starts a sort of chain reaction. Don't ask me why or how, but we are number four in less than that many months."

"So, the unmated males are hoping one of the women might be theirs?"

"Most of them, yes."

"Men actually looking for a commitment, that's is unusual."

"Not really, we live a long time. Finding a partner, a true mate, is the goal of most shifters, male and female. Not all of us are blessed with a true mate."

"That's why you decided to date so many women at the same time, because you were hoping to find a mate?"

"I was hoping to find a mate eventually. I knew none of the woman I was seeing was the one. I didn't want anyone to get the idea that I was mate material. Not all matings are true. They all knew I was not seeing them exclusively."

"Cora didn't get the memo."

"As I said, I think that had more to do with you being human than anything else."

"She was pretty clear that she thought you were hers."

"She was wrong and it will cost her her life for what she did to you."

"I'm not sure how I feel about her being put to death, but I do know I need to be sure she can't ever get near any of us ever again."

"She threatened my mate. She nearly took your life from you. She left you to die. She deserves death," Nico growled.

Emerald wasn't going to argue. Cora being dead would assure her that the woman never threatened her or her family again.

The sound of a vehicle coming up her driveway was loud and clear.

Nico held her, sneaking a quick kiss before she opened the door.

"Do you know who it is?" Emerald suddenly worried as she grabbed the door handle. It wasn't as if Cora was going to drive up to the front door, but Emerald still needed to be more cautious.

"It's Blythe, Ellery, Aya, and Tasha. Gwen, of course, is with them too. Jett is the guard with them."

"You can tell all of that without looking?"

"No, I can tell it because that's who Blythe said was coming," Nico smiled.

"Will you look at this place. How does an Assistant to the Mayor afford a place like this?" Tasha exclaimed, not realizing that Emerald could hear everything the group was saying.

Because of her new Shifter hearing, Emerald heard every word. Opening the door, she smiled. She knew what the old Manor house had looked like when she first saw it . Now, with new siding and the lawn manicured, it was impressive.

"Mommy, I gots litter pingers." Gwen showed off a new polish job.

"Yes, you do. They are very sparkly."

"Daddy, I made you a pitcher." Gwen had drawn an oval, sort of, with four stick legs and a long neck, topped with a circle. It looked like a spider.

"It's beautiful. You can tell me all about it."

"It a Shipper wolf," Gwen whispered but forgot to turn down the volume.

"She was looking at the books about Local legends this morning," Blythe quickly added.

"Oh, I love it. It's the best drawing I ever got. We can put it on the fridge, okay?"

The three-year-old nodded her head and rushed to the kitchen after hugging her mother.

"I'm going hang this up, then I will put something on for her to watch," Nico smiled, following the toddler into the other room.

"Alright, spill," Tasha said, glancing behind Emerald to make sure that Nico was gone.

"Spill?" Emerald didn't want to assume she knew what Tasha wanted to know.

"Since when is Tall, dark, and dangerous Gwen's Daddy?"

"It's a recent occurrence. We sort of eloped." Emerald used that as an excuse that the Human women would understand.

"Sort of?" Aya tilted her head, waiting for more.

"Yes."

"That's why one of his ex's attacked you?"

"Apparently, she didn't take the news well."

"How are you feeling?"

"I am much better now, thank you."

Emerald had actually suffered a concussion in Grade school when playing baseball. The batter threw the bat after hitting the ball and she was hit, resulting in six stitches and a concussion. She used that memory to describe to the women what she had felt. She hated lying. This wasn't a lie that would hurt anyone, but it still felt wrong.

23

Emerald looked to Ellery as she gave the women a tour of her expansive home.

"Do you smell that?" she asked Ellery since she was also newly turned by her mate, Eli.

"Skunk?" Ellery nodded.

"It smells like it's really close. It could be in the yard. I thought that skunks were nocturnal."

"I couldn't say. I know nothing about skunks other than they stink. Maybe, we should shut the windows," Ellery suggested as Aya and Tasha were still marveling at the enormous bathroom off of the hallway.

Nico was in the Living room with Gwen, Blythe, and Jett. Ellery was in the bedrooms shutting the windows with Emerald. The two Human women were just coming out into the hallway, but Emerald sensed nine heartbeats.

Her wolf was on high alert, eight people, nine heartbeats. Nico had taught her the skill of distinguishing each beat so she could assure herself that no one else was in her home. This ninth beat was not inside but close.

The Human women coming closer prevented Emerald from calling out to Ellery and asking her how many she heard.

"Are you okay?" Aya asked.

"I'm good," Emerald lied. This Ellery noticed.

"Did you girls check out the other rooms? There's a lot of them," Ellery asked.

"I thought it would be rude."

"Go ahead and explore," Emerald said, waving them off. "I'm going to shut the rest of these windows."

"It is getting skunky in here." Aya pinched her nose to accentuate the fact that they smelled it too.

"What's wrong?" Ellery asked Emerald as soon as the other two were out of earshot.

"I heard nine heartbeats, but there are only eight people."

Ellery stopped to listen then nodded. The sound drew both of them to the window they had just shut.

There on her back lawn, at the tree line, stood Cora.

"Oh shit," Ellery exclaimed.

"She's back to make sure I'm dead." Emerald noticed the words were more growl than actual words.

"Emerald, stay here. I'll get Nico."

"No, she's mine." Emerald's body was practically vibrating. She didn't wait for Ellery's further objection. She rushed down the stairs and out through the kitchen.

Nico and Jett were alerted to her quick movement but hadn't noticed why she was running outside.

"Stay away from my family." Emerald wasn't sure that her words were even words right now. She was half-shifted, her claws out, and her wolf pushing for more.

"He turned you! "Cora screeched, looking slightly nervous and smelling of skunk. The woman shifted, her clothing exploding off of her as she took a defensive stance.

She had masked her scent by rolling in it or something. That was how she had evaded the guards searching for her.

"Emerald?" Nico called, running toward them, but it was too late. Emerald's wolf was done being the victim. The shift was quick and painless, even in clothing.

In seconds, Emerald had a stunned Cora by the throat. The taste of skunk and her blood in her mouth didn't deter her.

Cora submitted, rolling onto her back, hoping for mercy.

"Emerald, you have the right to end her. I just worry how that will affect you in time."

Emerald tightened her jaws and the whimpering wolf beneath her stilled, waiting for the killing blow.

Nico was right. She wasn't worth it. If Cora needed to die, she wasn't going to be the one to do it. The satisfaction of having this monster at her mercy was enough for now.

"Sir," Jett said, pointing to the forest. A man with a wolf by his side stood on the edge.

"Emerald, Ghost, and Chance will take her. Jett is here with us. You can let go. She can't get away now."

Emerald sat back on her haunches, releasing the wolf, daring her to make a move. Cora didn't move at all. Emerald was wondering if she had actually killed the woman.

Chance, a man she had meant once, looked at her and dipped his chin. Taking prey away from a wolf was dangerous.

Emerald shifted back, looking down at Cora. "You're not worth it. Have a good time in hell," Emerald said as Ghost shifted back to his Human form and helped his brother drag the squirming wolf into the forest.

Ellery ran out, shoving clothing at Emerald, looking back at the house and the bedroom windows that faced the backyard.

"Where's Gwen?" Emerald asked, looking at the spot where Ghost and Chance had taken the wolf away.

"Blythe has her. Are you alright? Did you get hurt?"

"No, I didn't get hurt. I'm fine. I almost killed her. I could have killed her, Nico." Emerald was shaking as she got dressed.

"I know and you had the right to kill her."

"I'm glad you stopped me. Watching her shrink back and the fear in her eyes made me feel slightly vindicated. I don't know if I could live with taking another's life, even Cora's."

"We should go back inside. Aya and Tasha will wonder what's going on."

"Do you think they saw anything?"

"I don't think so. Tasha would be out here screaming her head off if she did."

"Maybe, you're right."

"Emerald, you're still shaking," Ellery said, walking with her back into the open kitchen door with Jett and Nico trailing.

"You'd be shaking too," Emerald laughed. "Now, help me figure out how to explain that I'm wearing different clothing."

"And you smell a little like skunk," Nico looked apologetically at her.

"I do. I need a shower."

"I'd say you need more than one," Ellery laughed.

"Nico, can you handle the women?"

"Yes, go take a shower. The smell is so strong I swear I can taste it."

"What the hell did she roll in?" Jett said as Emerald ran up the stairs, hoping that the women were still on their independent tour of the bedrooms so she could sneak into the bathroom.

24

Emerald showered twice before the smell faded to a tolerable level. The women were leaving as she came down the stairs.

"I'm so sorry. I was not a very good host today," she said while walking them to the door.

"You shouldn't chase skunks," Tasha looked at her like she was a crazy person.

"I have learned that the hard way," Emerald sighed

"Say goodbye to Gwen for us. She fell asleep on the couch," Aya smiled.

"I will and thank you both for helping Ellery with Gwen. I was in no condition to care for her myself."

"Anytime, she's a hoot. She told us her Daddy is a shitter."

"A shipper," Nico corrected. I dabble in the Shipping industry."

"Of course, that makes perfect sense. We will stop by another time, if you're up to it," Aya said softly with a hint of sarcasm.

"You are always welcome."

"The Bed and Breakfast is lovely, but I'm sick of the same four walls. We have to be escorted everywhere," Aya looked at Jett like it was his fault.

"The woods are not safe unless you know them."

"Unless we know the woods or unless we know what's in them?" Tasha snaped back.

"Both," Jett responded.

"I'm sure the woods are full of terrifying things like rabid squirrels and other woodland creatures."

"Don't forget skunk," Blythe added, hoping to cut the tension.

Emerald looked at Nico. She was starting to wonder if the women had seen something. They were acting strange. In the end, she decided that Tash was not one to hold back a thought. She would have mentioned seeing a Wolf shifter on the back lawn.

"Gwen, Nico, and I would welcome your company. You should come for dinner, maybe next week? Ask Sarina and Mary Grace to come along."

"I think we might take you up on that. I'm glad to see you are recovered. We were worried."

"So was I," Nico smiled his signature *"Make women swoon"* smile.

Jett held the door for Aya, who glared at him, then Tasha, who did the same. Blythe rode in the front with Jett as Ellery sat in back with the two Human women she had been friends with since third grade.

"Was it me or were they acting strange?"

"I think it was us that were acting strange and they picked up on it," Nico replied. "They think you went out to confront a skunk."

"In a way, I did," Emerald laughed, shutting the door.

"How did you know it was Cora and not an actual skunk?"

"Nine heartbeats, eight people, then I saw her out in the yard. I can't believe she came back to make sure I was gone."

"She's insane, Emerald."

"I feel sort of bad. If she's truly insane, is she really responsible for her actions?"

"She is responsible."

"I know the witches mind-wiped the women at the Bed and Breakfast so they didn't remember even their own families. Can we do that to Cora?"

"You want to have her wiped instead of killed?"

"I don't know."

"Emerald, I love that you're so compassionate, but the woman tried to kill you. She left you for dead and came back to make sure you were gone. The mind wipe almost killed the women at the B&B. That's why the Pack rescued the six of them from the hospital."

"I was just trying to find a way to be sure she wouldn't come back."

"She's not ever coming back. Ghost and Chance have her. Blake will be her judge and jury."

"You were right when you said I would now have the upper hand. I took her down easily."

"I never doubted it."

"Mommy, I hungry," Gwen's sleepy voice made both of them turn.

Emerald had missed her daughter. The thought that Cora was never going to threaten her family ever again comforted her in a way she hadn't known she needed. She'd always count heartbeats and jump at shadows. In time, she might relax, but by then, Gwen would be a teenager, giving her a whole new set of worries.

"How does grilled cheese sound?" Emerald scooped her daughter into a big hug.

"I like gwilled cheese. Daddy, you want gwilled cheese?" Gwen looked lovingly at a man they had both come to love.

"Absolutely, Gwennie." Nico intercepted the three-year-old as she lunged at him from Emerald's arms.

Nico seemed to fit in immediately. It didn't feel strange at all to have him there with her and Gwen. "Blake called to see how we are doing," he announced, coming into the kitchen where Emerald was doing the lunch dishes. She was not going to let Cora's crime keep her from enjoying her new kitchen.

"We, as in you and me?"

"We, as in all of us, I told him that my mate and daughter were just fine and that we'd see them tomorrow. I assumed you'd be going to work. I'm sure he would give you time off, if you need it."

"I will be going to work. I want to stop in and see the ladies at the B&B as well. I feel like I was not a very good host to them."

"They didn't expect you to entertain."

"I know, but I would like to invite them to dinner next week to make up for it."

"Let's make it a party, our Mating party."

"Nico, they didn't know about shifters or mating. They looked suspicious that I was dating you."

"I will make sure to get down on one knee and make it official. Anyone else we decide to include will behave. It's not like we randomly shift for fun at parties."

"It would be a nice trick."

"It would solve the humans not knowing problem, that's for sure."

"Alright, a party would be nice. I haven't been to a real party since Alice and Blake mated."

"This place is plenty big enough. Speaking of which, I hope you don't mind, but I have Jett delivering my things this afternoon."

"You couldn't get them yourself?"

"I couldn't leave you and Gwen, not after Cora showed up."

"She's gone. She's never coming back."

"Damn right, I still don't know if you are up to being left alone here yet?"

"I don't know either. Maybe, you are right? It's too soon."

"Most newly Mated couples disappear for days when first mated."

"We don't have that luxury. Gwen was already away from home for two days, Nico."

"I wasn't suggesting we run away, Emerald. I am planning to stay by your side when you are not at work. I am sure that the threat is gone. I just like the idea of having a mate at my side."

"As well as a three-year-old?" Emerald pointed to Gwen, who was trying to shove an obviously wrong puzzle piece into an empty space on her floor puzzle.

"As soon as the three-year-old is asleep, I plan on making sure she gets a little brother or sister as soon as possible." Nico wagged his eyebrows, making Emerald laugh.

"I am all for expanding out little family, but I'm just getting used to the idea that I have a mate, one that's going to stick around for a while."

"I'm sticking around forever, Emerald, and nine months is probably enough time for you to get used to Mated life. Gwen has already adapted."

"Yes, she has. What time is it?"

"Four thirty, why?" Nico asked.

"Gwen doesn't go to bed for hours and she just took a nap."

"Does this mean you don't want to wait to start that family right away?" Nico smirked, knowing the answer.

"I don't want to wait for Gwen to fall asleep. I'd actually like to start right now," Emerald smiled.

"How long is a Princess movie?" Nico asked.

"Not long enough, we need something that will keep her attention for a while. Gwen, do you want to watch <u>Pooh</u> or <u>Shrek</u>?"

"Swek," Gwen exploded with excitement.

Emerald put the movie on and sat Gwen on the couch with a drink.

"That was some reaction," Nico smiled as Emerald glanced back to make sure Gwen was fully engaged.

"I have a small reserve of special movies that I don't let her watch all the time. She hasn't seen this in a while. We should have a while before she gets bored."

"How long do we have?"

"Maybe twenty minutes, we have to be quick."

"I can be quick, but later will be a different story."

"Nico, we are down to nineteen minutes."

"I'm right behind you," Nico smiled, following his mate up to their room.

Emerald was still feeling guilty.

"The doors are locked. You will hear her if she calls for us. Count the heartbeats, Emerald."

"Three," she smiled.

"Now, let's make it four."

If you enjoyed reading Nico and Emerald's story, please consider leaving a review? Reviews are the life's blood of the independent author.

Just Howl is Book 4 in my Blue Rock Shifters series.

Who is next? Will the other humans discover the truth? I'm working on Book 5 already, but you'll have to wait to find out whose book it is. I really love these characters and hope you do too. I hate to see the Three Packs series come to a close, so it looks like Blue Rock might be a long one. Hop over to my Facebook page and let me know whose story you want to read.

I appreciate all of my readers and would love to hear your opinions, good or bad. All suggestions are welcome. You can find me on my Facebook page, Paranormal Twist, for information and updates and to see what's next.

Turn the page for a list of other books and series available now.

Other series by Lynn Leite:
Moon Valley shifters
Pack
On Tour (Contemporary Romance)
Dragon Fire
Undying
Ridgeland Bears
Howlin Ranch
Shifted
Bitten
Ascension
Spark
Omega
Sierra Moon
You can find these and other stand-alone books on Amazon. As always, thank you for reading. Your ratings and comments are much appreciated.

Happy reading, Lynn Leite.

www.ingramcontent.com/pod-product-compliance
Lightning Source LLC
Chambersburg PA
CBHW061258120726

48001CB00001B/358